Villa Kalman's Secrets

Rachele Modiano Mendes - The Early Years
Book 2

Silvano Stagni

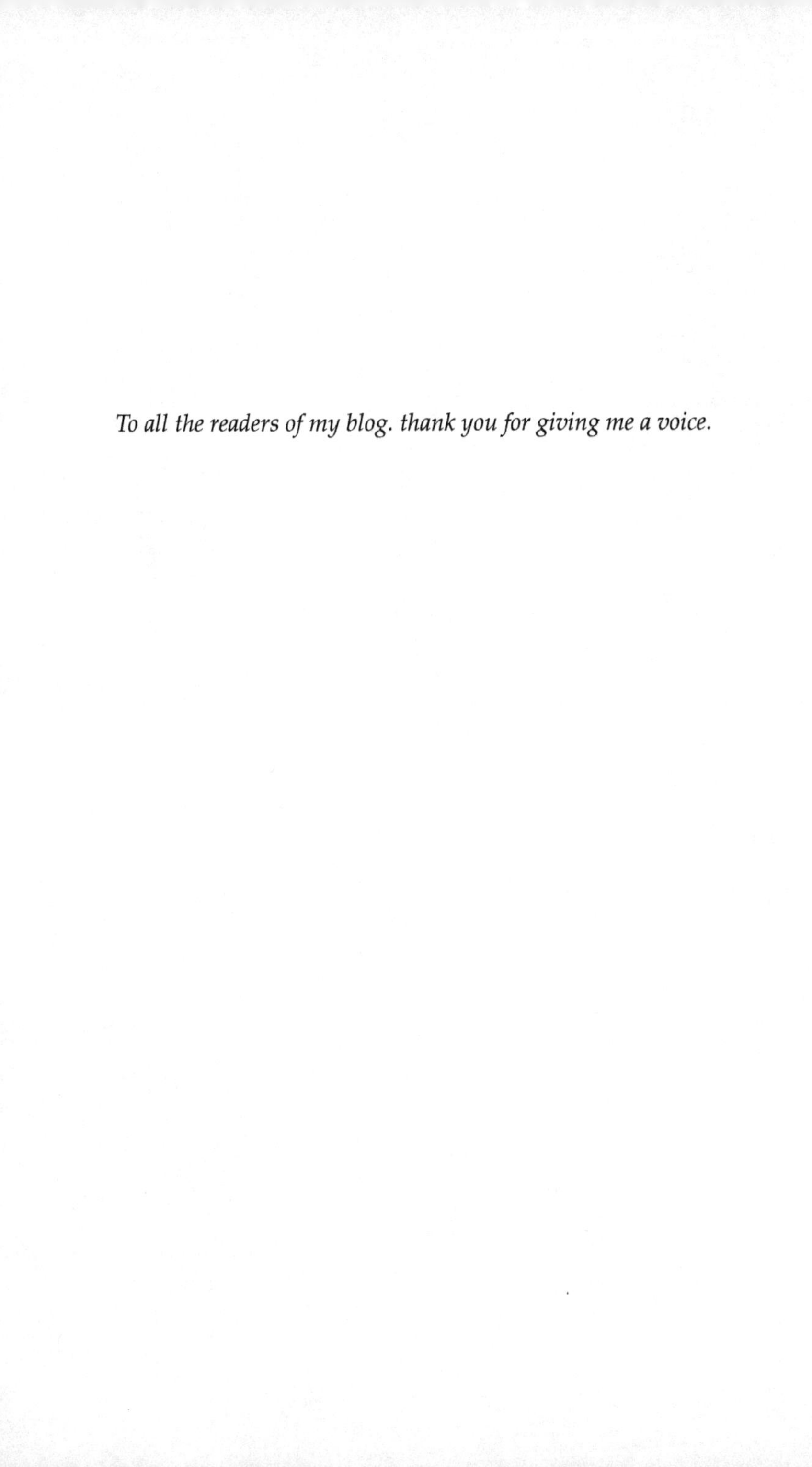

To all the readers of my blog. thank you for giving me a voice.

Also by Silvano Stagni

Reflections in the Water

1921. Rachele Modiano starts working for a Venetian law firm after she married Gabriele Mendes. Her first case turns into a web of fraud, blackmail, and possibly murder. Rachele must win over a magistrate, who dismisses her as an aristocrat toying with the law as a hobby, and protect her client's name.

Book 1 of the series Rachele Modiano Mendes - The Early Years

The Dressmaker's Parcels

The story of the Modiano Mendes clan during Mussolini's racial laws, World War II, and the Holocaust. Spoiler: Rachele and her eldest daughter Emma join the resistance.

Available on Amazon

Elena's Memory

Venice, 1947. The search for the legitimate heir to a couple who did not survive the camps brings a young woman who lost her memory to Venice. The love and support of the extended Modiano-Mendes clan helps her recover her memory. They soon realise that the attempts to get rid of her had nothing to do with the inheritance.

Book 1 of the series: Rachele Modiano Mendes investigates

Available on Amazon

Unconditional

A collection of feel-good short stories about acceptance, love, and memories.

Foreword

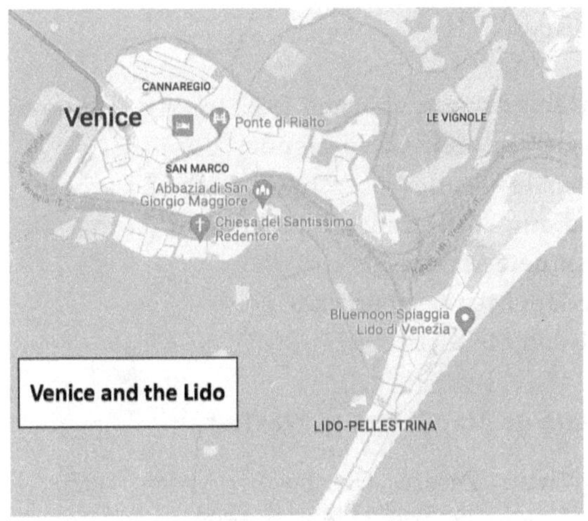

Map Courtesy of Google Maps

Each series has repeated characters. Five families feature in the series. As time goes by, children are born and family members are lost because they move away or die. Here are the four families at the beginning of the story, in 1925.

Gabriele Mendes, Paolo Mondani, and Alvise Cantoni met in primary school when they were 6 and have been friends ever since. Paolo Mondani was 'emotionally adopted' by the Mendeses after his parents died. Arrigo thinks of Samuele and Fiamma as his grandparents and the Mendes siblings as his uncles and aunts.

The Mendes family from Venice

Samuele Mendes (born 1870), married **Fiamma Andrade** (born 1873) in 1894

- **Raffaele Mendes** (born in 1895), married **Antonella Levi – Children: Carlo Mendes,** born 1923
- **Gabriele Mendes** (born 1897), married **Rachele Modiano - Children: Emma Mendes** (born 1924)
- **Emanuele Mendes** (born 1902)
- **Myriam Mendes** (born 1905),
- **Roberto Mendes** (born 1913)

The Pesaro de Bonfili family (Venice)

Count Victor Pesaro De Bonfili (born 1865), **Deborah Camerini** (born 1873) – married in 1898

- **Giorgio Pesaro De Bonfili** (born 1902)
- **Sarah Pesaro De Bonfili** (born 1905)

The Modiano family from Trieste

Baron Davide Modiano (born in 1860) married **Esther Coronel** (born in 1866) in 1884.

- **Greta Modiano** (b. 1885), married **Michele Treves – they made alyah three months after Emma Mendes was born (May 1924).** (Children not mentioned in the book)
- **Michele Modiano** (born 1887), married **Stella Basevi** - Children: **Maximilian Modiano** (b. 1912), **Paola Modiano** (b.1915), **Alex Modiano** (b. 1919)
- **Sarah Modiano** (born 1888), married to **Hans Basevi** - (Children not mentioned in the book)
- **Celeste Modiano** (born 1890), married to **Maximilian Attard** - (Children not mentioned in the book)
- **Daniele Modiano** (born 1891), will marry **Perla Oppenheim**
- **Ricardo Modiano** (born 1894), married to **Hannah Sarah Cohen** - (Children not mentioned in the book)
- **Rachele Modiano** (born 1898), married to **Gabriele Mendes**
- **Barbara Modiano (born 1900),** married to **Herbert Cohen.**

The Cantoni Family (Venice)

Alvise Cantoni – (born in 1897), married to **Viola Luzzato** (born in 1899)

- **Franco** (born in 1924)

The Mondani Family (Venice)

Paolo Mondani – (born in 1897) married to **Sofia Taiman** (born in 1899)

* **Arrigo** (born in 1918)

Other recurring characters

Anita Torgnon – Gabriele and Rachele's live-in housekeeper and Rachele's close friend and confidante. She is considered an integral part of the Mendes family and is always included in family events.

Franco Venier – One of the founding partners of the Venier-Zanin law firm, he is Rachele's boss

Chapter One

September 1925

Sunday, 13 September 1925

It was a nice summer day in September. Late August rains ensured that the oppressive heat and humidity of a Venetian summer were gone. Bianca Volpato was watching her grandson and a few friends play volleyball in the back garden. The net was a rope tied to a tree on one side and a pole in the fence on the other. As they were playing, they were talking about what they would do with themselves during the last couple of weeks of school holidays. One boy dived and caught the ball using his fists. Unfortunately, he threw it back very high and it landed on the other side of the fence.

Since the Hotel Excelsior opened in 1908, developers built several upmarket Villas in that part of the Lido of Venice between the Hotel and the lagoon. Villa Kalman was built on the side of a canal. The area was not completely developed and still had a few more humble old houses. Bianca Volpato's husband had refused to sell his land to developers, and the property was now between two liberty-style villas. They knew that the owners of Villa Kalman had left for Vienna. Bianca's grandson decided to climb the fence to retrieve the ball. He had helped the Villa's temporary staff carry or retrieve things from boats moored at the nearby pier and knew how to open the side gate to leave once he had found the ball. A friend, a promising gymnast, helped him climb the fence.

They found the ball, but before they could open the back gate, somebody started shooting from the house. The two teenagers found the button to open the gate and ran out. It was only when they were outside that one of them realised the cartridge must have grazed his leg. The wound was not even bleeding, or at least not yet. Bianca had come out of the kitchen when she heard the shots. She saw her grandson's friend's leg, went back inside, and reappeared with a bag containing disinfectant and bandages. A retired midwife, she dressed the wound. The volleyball match was forgotten. The other boys were trying to find out what had happened. Bianca was listening in the background, wondering who could have shot from the Villa when it was supposed to be empty.

Except the villa was not empty. The owner had asked the manager of the Hotel Excelsior if he knew somebody who could stay in the villa until they would be back in the summer. He had introduced him to Dario Zago, the son of one of the senior members of his team. The first in his extended family to attend university, he was the oldest of six children, and needed a quiet place to study that was better than the hotel boiler room. Dario heard the shots as well and wondered where they were coming from. He took his caretaking duties seriously and started inspecting the Villa from the top floor since he was occupying two rooms that the architect had meant as servant's quarters. He was concentrating on finding signs that somebody had been in the house, so he did not hear the back gate being opened and closed. By the time he had inspected the first floor and the raised ground floor, he noticed the time. He was not in his mother's good books because he had skipped church to study, and could not be late for Sunday lunch. He checked that the main door did not have any sign of forced entry, left from the backdoor planning to check the kitchen, staff rooms and basement when he came back.

20 September 1925

Rachele Modiano Mendes had arrived in synagogue later than she used to before she had a daughter. Emma was 19 months and she could already walk. However, the walk between their home in Campo San Giacomo dall'Orio and the Synagogue was too long for a toddler. She had to be carried for most of the way. Gabriele, Rachele's husband, had asked Anita, their very protective housekeeper, to walk with her. Anita was not Jewish, but after three years working for the Mendeses, she had become part of the family and was never left out of any big celebration or family gathering. She knew Rachele was three months pregnant and her husband was keen she did not carry their daughter for longer periods. They would tell the family during lunch; until then, the official excuse was that she was invited to lunch, so it was easier for everybody if she joined them in synagogue.

Rachele's mother-in-law, Fiamma Andrade Mendes, and Deborah Camerini, Countess Pesaro De Bonfili, had been close friends since they started primary school. They were honorary aunts to the other one's children. They had Friday night dinners and Saturday lunches together every other week. That week it was the Pesaro de Bonfili's turn to host. So, at the end of the service, the whole Mendes clan was walking to the home of Count Pesaro de Bonfili. Rachele was waking next to the countess.

"Aunt Deborah, should I be worried that you have made an appointment to come and see me at work on Monday morning?"

Rachele did not like to talk about work during the Sabbath or religious holidays. So her honorary aunt was vague.

"It is not for me. It is one of my clients who may or may not need your help. I thought it was easier if I made the appointment."

Rachele noticed that her honorary aunt did not provide any detail. It was the second day of Rosh Hashanah, the Jewish New Year, so she did not like to talk about work. Either Countess Deborah agreed or she had trained her well. Her nephew Carlo, three years old, tripped while negotiating the steps of a bridge across a narrow canal. The Countess instinctively started rushing forward to pick him up, but she stopped when she saw her daughter and her honorary niece Myriam Mendes had got to Claudio before her. They checked he had not hurt himself, then Myriam picked him while her daughter was making funny faces to make him stop crying. The countess turned to wait for Rachele to catch up with her.

"Whenever you need help with Emma, you just need to ask. Half of us will be available, but, remember, those two may run faster than their mothers, but Fiamma and I come first."

Rachele nodded. She and Gabriele had planned to announce the new pregnancy before it was time to recite the blessing after the meal.

21 September 2021

Gabriele and Rachele did not make many changes to the morning routine after the birth of their first daughter. They used their income to invest in further help to allow Anita to dedicate time to Emma when Rachele was working. Rachele's older sisters had similar arrangements, so their parents expected nothing else. Gabriele's parents accepted it, although the jury was still out on whether they approved it. His sister, Myriam, liked it because it would pave the way for her to have similar arrangements later in life when she had a family.

Usually, Rachele and Gabriele alternated supervising Emma's breakfast before going to work. That meant Emma had been trained to have early nights and early mornings. She was not keen to wake up, in the same way that in the first few months of her life, she was not that keen to fall asleep. Gabriele and Rachele would still walk together to her office, and then Gabriele would continue to his office. That morning, they talked about their family's reaction to their second pregnancy. Gabriele was feeling overprotective.

"Everyone knows you are pregnant. They will be more inclined to help."

They had avoided walking past the Rialto fish market. The smell of fish made Rachele queasy.

"I am not sure things will change. Even now I get to hold Emma after Anita, Fiamma, and Aunt Deborah are done with her."

Gabriele noticed a new shop selling children's clothes just past Campo San Polo, he made a note of the location to come back later to buy Emma's first winter coat, hoping that grandparents or great uncles and aunts (honorary or not) would not buy it before him.

"She is ours first thing in the morning, before her bedtime, and on Shabbat afternoon. "

Rachele replied in a teasing tone in her voice.

"Unless grandparents or great uncle and aunts come to visit. "

Gabriele felt the need to justify his honorary aunt.

"Aunt Deborah is dying to become a grandmother, but Giorgio and Sarah are not married yet. She is pouring all her frustrated grandmotherly love towards Carlo and Emma. When are we telling Paolo and Sofia?"

Paolo Mondani was one of Gabriele's closest and oldest friends. They met on the first day of school when they were six and had been friends ever since.

"When do you have time to see them?"

"They would know now if we had told everybody the first day rather than the second. We could invite them for coffee or whatever Saturday afternoon."

They were crossing Rialto Bridge; they stopped at the top. Rachele loved looking at the Canal Grande from the top of the bridge. She called it her Canaletto moment. After four and a half years in Venice, it had not grown old yet. When they started walking away from the view Rachele loved so much, she turned to her husband.

"This evening, I shall call Sofia to invite them."

When they reached the door to Rachele's office, Gabriele kissed his wife and started walking to his office. As usual, Rachele looked at her husband before turning around and climbing the stairs to the first floor where the offices of the Venier-Zanin law firm were.

When she arrived, the receptionist told her that her first appointment had arrived early. Rachele walked into the meeting room. Countess Deborah introduced her to her client, the manager of Hotel Excelsior, one of the most expensive hotels at the Lido. She excused herself, saying she just had to go to her office to put down her handbag and collect her notepad. On her way out, she asked a secretary to organise refreshments for the visitors.

Ten minutes later, Rachele was back. The receptionist had brought three coffee cups. She had gone off coffee but had not yet told her boss she was pregnant again. However, her honorary aunt knew.

"Rachele, do you want me to drink your coffee?"

"Yes, please. I feel ridiculous to have gone off coffee. After all, I am a Modiano!"

Countess Pesaro de Bonfili felt the need to include an explanation in the introduction.

"Rachele, this is Mario Dolfin, the manager of the Hotel Excelsior. I regularly scout paintings for the hotels. Last week he asked me if I knew a discrete lawyer, so here we are. Mario, this is Avvocato Rachele Modiano Mendes."

Rachele and Mario Dolfin bowed their heads to acknowledge the introduction.

"Are you related to Michele Modiano? We buy our coffee from Maxtor."

"He is my brother. He works with our father in the family business, coffee trading, and had the idea of creating a small coffee roasting company, Maxtor. My great-grandfather started importing coffee in Trieste and selling it to coffee roasting companies all over Europe."

Rachele moved the tray with the coffees away from her.

"It is embarrassing that the smell of coffee makes me queasy. It did not happen during my previous pregnancy."

Mario Dolfin wanted to be sympathetic, but he was aware a man's sympathy has limits when dealing with a pregnant woman.

"I have three children. If I remember correctly, my wife's pregnancies were all different. But what do I know? I am a man."

Rachele thought it was time to find out why Mario Dolfin needed discrete legal advice. She expected it would be something embarrassing. She opened her notepad.

"What brought you here, Mr Dolfin? Why did you not go to the Hotel's legal advisor?"

Mario Dolfin did not sound embarrassed at all.

"Let's start with the second question. I am interested in finding a different legal advisor. Avvocato Manin retired last June, and he left his law firm to his nephew, who is not as good as his uncle. However, this does not concern the hotel. Two fairly senior members of staff independently shared a story asking for my help. At the end, I realised their sons were part of the same event."

He then told the story of what happened when two teenagers jumped the fence of Villa Kalman to retrieve their ball.

"Dario Zago swore to me and to his father that he was not the shooter. He did not know there was a rifle in the Villa. The accountant that takes care of the Italian financial interests of the owner of Villa Kalman reported the two boys to the police for attempted theft."

Rachele stopped taking notes.

"You said that Dario Zago was the only occupier of the Villa."

Mario Dolfin took out a folded piece of paper from the inside pocket of his jacket. He opened it, revealing notes.

"I spoke to Dario before asking Countess Pesaro de Bonfili to recommend a lawyer. He said that he was late for Sunday lunch and he did not check the lower ground floor and the basement. When he went back, he noticed that the back door was ajar. He was sure he had closed it and locked it from the outside."

Rachele finished writing.

"What would you like me to do?"

"The two teenagers and the young man are all accused of something. Can you help them? Their parents are not wealthy, but we could use the special personal emergency funds to which all the hotel staff contribute."

"I need to talk to them before accepting. I will also talk to my boss to see if we can take it pro-bono or at a discount. Speaking of my boss, would you consider us as your next legal advisor? That might give me a reason to ask to work on a pro-bono or discounted basis. I also would like to stress that I appreciate there may be other firms in the running."

Mario Dolfin liked the professional demeanour of the person on the other side of the table. He almost forgot he was dealing with a woman, and a pregnant woman at that.

"I have been favourably impressed by what I have seen and heard so far."

Rachele stood up

"Let me see if my boss, Avvocato Franco Venier, is free. I would like you to meet him. While you talk to him, I shall check my diary and pencil in three possible dates and time to see Dario Zago and the boys. I have to meet the boys with at least one of their parent, so I may come to the Lido one Sunday if you are so kind to find a room in your hotel where we can have a private conversation."

Mario Dolfin agreed to meet Franco Venier. Rachele left the room, hoping she could come back with him.

Chapter Two

September 1925

23 September 1925

Franco Venier had agreed to operate pro-bono for the two teenagers and at a huge discount for Dario Zago. He reckoned it was the way for the law firm to gain the trust of Mario Dolfin and stand a chance to become the legal advisors for the Hotel Excelsior. That morning, Rachele was supposed to meet Dario Zago and sign him up as a client. She had finished giving breakfast to Emma and was now trying to brush her teeth before dressing her for the day. Emma did not like the toothbrush, she liked it even less when it was in her mouth. Brushing her teeth was a battle of wills between mother and daughter. Halfway through the battle, Rachele thought of what she had told Mario Dolfin. The next two Sundays were Jewish Holidays, so she could not talk to the boys and their parents. She stopped brushing Emma's teeth. Her daughter smiled, thinking she won the battle. Rachele called Gabriele and asked him to write a note to call Mario Dolfin about Sundays and leave it by her briefcase so she would see it before going to work. Much to the surprise of her daughter, Rachele went back to brushing her teeth. Emma was clearly disappointed. What she thought was a victory had proven to be only a truce.

~

When Rachele called the hotel Excelsior, they told her that Mario Dolfin was out and they expected him back in the afternoon, after the lunch break. Rachele did not expect to see him with Dario Zago when she walked into the meeting room, with a notepad and a folder with all the paperwork for new clients.

"Good morning, Avvocato Modiano. I shall meet your aunt in an hour. She has several painting she thinks I should see, so I came with Dario. His father was supposed to accompany him, but he couldn't swap his shift, so he asked me to come."

Rachele kept the social chitchat to a minimum, long enough to be polite. She wanted to take advantage of the opportunity to impress Mario Dolfin.

"We have agreed to submit the paperwork to take care of the two teenagers pro-bono, and charge Dario Zago only 25% of our rates. Based on what you told me, we reckon helping him will not take a lot of our time."

She turned to Dario Zago

"I need to go through some formalities, billing will not include this hour."

She took a form out of the folder.

"How old are you?"

"I turned 20 last July, I was born on July 15th, 1905 I am still a minor.[1] My father could not come, but he trusts Mario Dolfin. Whatever we discuss I will take the forms with me and return them tomorrow countersigned by him."

Once the formalities were over, Dario told Rachele what he did the previous Sunday after he heard the shots. Rachele kept taking notes. The interesting part came at the end.

"When I came back from lunch, I found the staff door ajar. I am pretty sure I double locked it on my way out. I inspected the kitchen, the staff hall, and storage on the lower ground floor, but the door to the basement was locked. Again, I am confident it did not use to be. I double checked the entire house again, but I found nothing out of place or any other sign people had been there."

Once he finished his tale. Dario looked at Rachele as if she had a solution to the problems he had not yet disclosed. Rachele looked at her notes. She had kept Mario Dolfin's notes from the previous meeting.

"Did you tell anybody about the staff door and the locked door to the basement?"

Dario was sitting in the same posture his primary school teacher told him to maintain when he was sitting at his desk.

"Yes, I told Gino Moras, the accountant of the owners of the villa."

"Did he do anything?"

"He told me it was not a problem. He had already told the police of the attempted theft. Which was news to me."

Mario Dolfin thought it was time to intervene.

"Gino Moras later called the police, saying that two teenagers had trespassed into the property, with the view to see if they could find something to steal. Those two teenagers were Bianca Volpato's grandson and his friend. The problem is that he reported the attempted entry when Dario was having lunch with his family. You can see what the two boys told me and the police in my notes."

Rachele found the lines in the notes that were mentioning the timescale according to the two boys.

"Bianca Volpato corroborates their timing, because she bandaged her grandson's friend's leg. Once the police talked to the boys, they accused Dario of shooting at them."

Rachele was still looking at Mario Dolfin's notes, the piece of paper was open and placed next to the notes she took. Dario Zago felt he had to say something.

"So, at the moment, I am accused of shooting at two trespassers, and I did not shoot anybody. The boys are accused of attempted theft, and they came into the garden just to retrieve their ball. Gino Moras has told the police a different version of the event."

Rachele felt she should be cautious

"Gino Moras could be in good faith. There is an unanswered question. If you did not shoot, but heard the shot, who did shoot? Also, according to Mr Dolfin's notes, Bianca Volpato treated a wound that was below the knee at an angle that made her think somebody fired the shot from a window on the lower ground floor or the basement. Can she be trusted?"

Mario Dolfin was confident she could. Her husband loved hunting and had a hunting rifle. She had treated more than one superficial wound caused by somebody being careless when they were carrying a rifle. Rachele looked at her notes.

"We will represent you, but as far as you have told me, Gino Moras and the police only have circumstantial evidence against you. The big question is, where did the shot come from and who fired the shot? Has anybody found the rifle?"

Dario and Mario Dolfin looked at each other. Dario felt he had to reply.

"Not until now, which is why I am being cautioned, not charged."

Rachele wrote something down in her notepad

"What about the boys? Where are they now?"

"For the moment, they were cautioned, but they had to stay at the Lido. "

Rachele looked at her watch. Time to close the meeting. There was nothing else she could learn now.

"I do not think this will become very expensive, Mr Zago. Please remember to take the forms with you and return them countersigned by your father. Then you will be my client. As things are now, I am not obliged to keep client confidentiality for anything concerning you."

The meeting was over. As they were leaving the meeting room, Rachele said to herself, more than to her visitors.

"Yes, the trick in this story is finding who shot at the two boys. Luckily, it will be difficult for the police as well."

As Rachele was seeing them out, she remembered the reason behind the earlier attempt to call Mario Dolfin. She asked him to organise a meeting with the boys and their parents for one evening that week or the following week around 5pm, and let her know. She also added that Friday was also not convenient for her.

It was Gabriele's turn to put Emma to bed. Somehow, they had fallen into a pattern without having discussed it. The first parent to wake up would sort out Emma for the day, the other parent would give her a bath and sort her out for the night. Rachele and Anita were in the kitchen sorting out dinner. Anita noticed Rachele had started making a cake, a sign she needed to relax.

"Is it anything you feel free to talk about?"

Rachele stopped kneading the dough for the cake.

"Anita, I think you and Gabriele must be the two people who know me best. I was thinking of two teenagers who jumped a fence to retrieve a ball, got shot at by a mysterious person, and are now accused of attempted theft. I cannot go into any more details."

Anita was putting a tray of vegetables in the oven, turning her back to Rachele. The two women were working well together in the kitchen. They could focus on what they were doing and talk to each other.

"I think I know enough to understand why you need to let off steam."

Rachele's emotional floodgates had opened.

"Maybe it is because I am more emotional than usual, but I want to find out who shot at them. I think somebody created the entire story of the attempted theft to divert attention from the shooter."

Anita was about to say something when Gabriele walked into the kitchen.

"Emma is asleep. We should be able to eat without interruption. Is there anything I can do to help?"

When they did not have guests, they would eat together in the kitchen. Anita had already laid the table. Rachele had started rolling the dough. She lifted her head.

"It is still warm for this time of the year. We could finish dinner with cake and something on the terrace. Why don't you make sure everything is ready for us to move there once we have finished eating?"

After dinner, Gabriele asked Anita if she minded looking after Emma for an hour. They did not walk home together after work. He wanted to go out for a walk with Rachele if she was not too tired. Before they left, Gabriele wheeled Emma's cot to the living room so Anita could be in the kitchen to clear out dinner and be able to hear Emma if she started crying.

There was very little Gabriele did not like about living in Venice. What he loved was walking around the city at night. Walking next to his wife in Venice at night, never failed to put him in a good mood. Silence between them felt intimate rather than heavy. Rachele had acquired the habit of transitioning from work to home, walking next to her husband. That day, she walked home alone, and missed walking alongside him. Gabriele had nothing specific to discuss, so he was just enjoying being next to his wife and wait for her to talk or for something he could point out to her. They were silent as they were walking along Calle Del Tentor. Something was bothering Rachele. She had not stopped to look at any of the shop windows along the street. When they were climbing the steps of a bridge, she turned to Gabriele.

"I wonder if being a mother and being pregnant plays a role in my reaction to what happened to two teenage boys who jumped a fence to retrieve a ball."

Gabriele looked at his wife, mocking a suffering face.

"I feel this is like chapter 10 of your train of thoughts. I need you to share the beginning if you want my opinion."

Rachele had to laugh. Her husband always teased her about starting conversations in her own head and speaking only after she had reached chapter four, confusing those who had just listened to what she said.

"I have done it again, haven't I?"

Rachele told Gabriele the story of the two boys and how she had to make sure they were legally protected from being accused of trying to steal from an empty villa. When she finished, Gabriele was quiet for a few minutes.

"I don't think it is because you are a mother. I have seen you deal with my younger siblings before you were pregnant with Emma. You are just a very caring person. Speaking of pregnancy, how are you? How do you feel about coping with your job, your husband, your daughter, and your pregnancy?"

Rachele kissed her husband's cheek and tightened her grip on his arm.

"I do not cope with you. I love every minute we spend together. As for everything else, I am grateful for whatever brought Anita into our lives. She and your mother are the pillars I keep leaning on to balance work, motherhood, and pregnancy."

24 September 1925

Rachele had just finished talking to the two teenagers and their families and was ready to go home. She was putting away her notepads in her briefcase when Mario Dolfin knocked at the doorpost of the open door..

"Thank you for letting me use your office. I will give it back to you in less than ten minutes. I just need to put things back in my briefcase and I am ready to go."

Mario Dolfin told her it did not matter, he just had to get his notebook to remind the staff of an important person due to arrive the following evening. He found it, then turned to Rachele.

"How did it go?"

Rachele kept putting things away.

"I talked to the two teenagers, and they gave a consistent story. Bianca Volpato corroborates their timing, and it also matches Dario Zago's version of the events. I am going to write a letter to the police stating that there is no ground to involve those two boys in any attempted theft."

"Bianca Volpato is well respected in the Lido of Venice. She delivered half the Venetian policemen working at the local police station. Her word will be taken very seriously. And Dario Zago?"

Rachele closed her briefcase.

"Things are circumstantial. We have his word that he locked the door and found it ajar. He says he was in his room on the second floor, and he was alone in the house. If he had hit the boy from the second floor, the wound would have been different. The boy's mother insisted he showed me the scar."

Mario Dolfin smiled

"So he is out of trouble as well."

"Not exactly. He says he was alone, but somebody used a hunting rifle to shoot at those two boys from the villa. Given that Dario Zago admits he only looked at the first floor and the raised ground floor, it is likely that the shooter was on the lower ground floor, a location that would match the shape and the position of the wound. The problem is finding evidence. Who called the police to inform them of an attempted theft?"

"I think it was Mr Kron's accountant in Venice, Gino Moras."

Rachele asked if she could take a sheet out of the notepad on Mario Dolfin's desk. She took a note of the name of the person who informed the police.

"I will have to talk to him. Please remind me who is Mr Kron."

"Laszlo Kron is the owner of Villa Kalman, a Hungarian who lives in Vienna."

"I will write a letter to the police here at the Lido and another one to Gino Moras, stating that there is no evidence tying those two boys to any attempted theft. They jumped the fence to retrieve a ball. They could be prosecuted for trespassing, but that would probably be considered a frivolous prosecution."

Rachele asked him if she could use the phone to call home and tell them she was about to leave the hotel. Mario Dolfin had no problem and left his office, leaving her space to make the call. He was waiting for her outside the door.

"Based on what I have seen so far, I like the way you work. Could you arrange a meeting with your boss? I'd like to talk to him about your firm becoming our legal advisors. Please do not celebrate yet. There are other Venetian law firms being considered. Meanwhile, one of the hotel speedboats will take you home. On behalf of those two families, thank you for coming."

Chapter Three

September-October 1925

28 September 1925

It was one of those times when Rachele thanked the almighty she had Anita in her life. Anita had sorted out the Mendes grandchildren's meal. She then had taken Emma and her cousin, little Claudio Mendes, to synagogue to allow her father-in-law, Samuele Mendes, to pass on the blessing of the Cohanim to his children and grandchildren. They were now walking to the home of Gabriele's parents, who lived close to the Synagogue, to have dinner. The Pesaro de Bonfili were also invited. Countess Pesaro de Bonfili walked next to Rachele.

"How are you getting on with Mario Dolfin?"

The holiday was over. Rachele could talk about work. She knew her aunt was well aware of that.

"I hope to sort out the two teenage boys during the week. I just need to talk to Gino Moras to see if he can withdraw the charge of attempted theft. If he can't, I will send a strongly worded 'lawyer's letter' to the investigating police department and to him. Tell me, did you know that the Hotel Excelsior was looking for a new legal advisor?"

They were now in the Campo del Ghetto Novo and were about to walk through the archway that lead to the bridge that would take them to Fondamenta del Ghetto and to Samuele and Fiamma's home where dinner was waiting after the long fast. The Countess noticed that Roberto Mendes held hands with his nephew Carlo, the son of his eldest brother Raffaele, while carrying Emma.

"Isn't Roberto very good with his nephew and niece? Mario Dolfin might have mentioned it. Why?"

"Last Thursday when I spoke to him he asked me to talk to my boss and prepare the paperwork, although he is looking at other law firms."

The Countess stopped walking. The light of a streetlamp was on her. Rachele could see she did not follow the rule not to use makeup on Yom Kippur.

"Do you want me to talk to him?"

Rachele realised the Countess had a plan when she came to see her with Mario Dolfin.

"Maybe. Can I let you know on Wednesday?"

30 September 1925

Rachele had sent a messenger to deliver a note to the address for Gino Moras that Dario Zago gave her. The message was written in the law firm letterhead and had a request to call her at his convenience before the end of the week. She was representing the two teenagers he had accused of attempted theft. She wanted to talk to him before writing to the police and the magistrate in charge of the attempted theft investigation. The letter had the effect she hoped, Gino Moras had rung the law firm as soon as he could.

"Thank you for your call, Mr Moras. I would like to come to the point quickly because I hate to waste your time. I have witnesses that corroborate the two teenagers' story that they jumped the fence to retrieve the ball. They were playing volleyball in the Volpato's garden."

Gino Moras was quiet for a few minutes.

"That is not the story I heard. "

Rachele was using her best 'lawyer's voice', the one she used when interrogating witnesses in court.

"May I ask you who told you? Dario Zago told me he did not call you. He heard the shot from his room on the second floor. The police agree with me that whoever shot the boys was shooting from the lower ground floor, otherwise the wound would be different."

"I do not feel free to tell you."

"I would also add that the police did not find any rifle in the Villa and that Bianca Volpato, one of the two teenagers' grandmother delivered the child of the head of the police station at the Lido, so he is inclined to believe her."

There was another pause at the other end.

"Well, in that case, I was misinformed, and I am prepared to withdraw the charge."

Rachele was not ready to sound reassuring.

"That is a smart move. I would also add that the court is too busy to take any charge of trespassing against my clients seriously. I also represent Dario Zago, who is accused of shooting, but we have not found the rifle."

This time, Gino Moras reacted quickly.

"I never said he did. "

"No, the police are investigating who shot the boys. Even if it had been an attempted theft, it would have been illegal to shoot them and the police don't have to wait for the two teenagers' parents to press charges before they investigate."

Rachele noticed that the pause at the other end was longer than expected.

"How can I help?"

"Dario Zago is consistently saying that, as far as he knew, he was the only occupier of Villa Kalman, but he suspects somebody else was in the Villa that day. Do you know anything about it?"

If Gino Moras had been in court or in Rachele's office, she would have noticed signs of nervousness. He kept his voice calm, or so he thought.

"I absolutely have no idea. Why should I?"

By now, Rachele had enough experience to sense he was hiding something.

"According to Dario Zago, you have a set of keys. He found the back door ajar and the gardener that comes twice a week only has the key for the back gate and the one for the garden shed. Not the key to the house."

Gino Moras sound slightly less confident.

"I do not know anything about it. Maybe somebody else has the keys."

Now Rachele definitely thought he was hiding something.

"I have requested that the police contact Mr Kron in Vienna to find out. It is in the interest of my client, Dario Zago."

Gino Moras tried to keep his voice steady.

"I understand, unfortunately I cannot help you."

Rachele played dumb.

"If you do not know, you do not know. Thank you for your time and thank you for withdrawing the charge against my two clients. I will check with the police at the beginning of next week."

Rachele hang up and thought that she would write a letter confirming their conversation, to make sure that Gino Moras would not forget about dropping the charge.

7 October 1925

Rachele was supervising Emma's breakfast, sitting next to her at the table by the window in the kitchen. Anita was looking at the pantry to see what she needed to buy later in the day. Emma never had problems eating, yet she was not a chubby toddler. Rachele kept telling her daughter to eat more slowly. Frustrated, she turned to Anita.

"Where do you think she puts what she eats? When we took her to Trieste before the holidays, my parents wondered whether we fed her properly."

Anita came out of the pantry, added a couple of items to her shopping list, and moved closer to Emma and Rachele.

"Did they still think so after they spent any time with her? Emma is a bundle of energy, aren't you, Emma? She only stays still when she sleeps or when she plays with her books."

Rachele thought Emma liked the colours of the picture books her Modiano grandparents had given her. She looked at the cupboard behind her mother, pointed at the book, making the two adults understand in no uncertain terms she wanted it. Rachele turned to Anita.

"You have uttered the magic word."

She looked at the kitchen clock, picked up the book, and started naming something in the picture and asking Emma where it was.

Gabriele walked into that domestic scene. Kissed his wife and his daughter on the forehead, sat at the table and realised he just had an empty plate. He stood up again.

"Anita, where are the biscuits?"

"Out of Emma's reach, she already had her breakfast."

She took the plates with the biscuits and put it on the table far from Emma, but close enough to Gabriele. She did the same with the cup of coffee.

"Is there anything special I should add to the shopping list?"

Gabriele and Rachele looked at each other. They both shook their heads. Anita went to check the cleaning cupboard. Gabriele reminded Rachele she had to get ready to go. They had to leave in less than half an hour. Rachele rolled her eyes, teasing him.

"It is just an excuse to spend time with your daughter."

Emma complained that her mother had to stop reading her book. Gabriele took over, feigning reluctance.

On their way to work, Gabriele had asked Rachele whether she had already told Franco Venier she was expecting a baby and that she was due the following February. That conversation was still in her mind when the receptionist came to tell her that Dario Zago had arrived and he was waiting for her in the smaller meeting room. She was on her way to sort out coffee and water for him. Rachele told her she already had too many coffees and declined any refreshments. She finished writing a note on the contract she was looking at, picked up the notepad marked 'Villa Kalman' and left her office.

When she walked into the meeting room, she caught Dario Zago pacing around the room. She wondered whether offering him coffee had been a good move. Maybe a hot chocolate would have been better. He did not even wait to be told to sit down.

"Yesterday, they informed me a magistrate would start looking into the shooting to see if there is any ground to charge me with attempted murder. I did not shoot anybody."

Rachele felt she had to calm him down.

"I wonder if they are using the threat to make you admit you shot the boys. Anyway, my boss, Avvocato Venier, is a close friend of a magistrate. If you allow me, I will ask Antonio Penzo for his opinion."

Unfortunately, she was not convincing enough.

"I am a second year law student, the first of my family to go to university. I do not need any flaw in my relationship with the law. I need to make sure I am cleared, even if they only charge me of shooting a rifle without a firearm licence. I am afraid that might create problems later when I want to find work as a lawyer."

Rachele tried again.

"It is not as big an offence as you think. It will not disqualify you from practicing law. However, I will do my best to help you. I have spoken to the boys. Are you sure you were alone in the Villa? Let's go through once again to what happened that Sunday morning."

Dario went through what he remembered. Rachele compared what she was hearing with her notes of their previous meeting. She stopped him after he told him he had locked the back door when he left the villa.

"Think back. What makes you so sure that you locked the door on your way out? It is important. Close your eyes, think of that moment."

Dario Zago closed his eyes for a few minutes.

"After I locked the door, I put my keys in the right-hand pocket of my trousers and I heard them when they hit the gravel. I did not realise my pocket had a hole, so I put them in my jacket pocket. I told my mother, and she told me to take my trousers off. She sorted out the hole in the pocket before lunch."

Rachele added that to her notes.

"You see, it was important. Now we are sure you double locked the door. It is only circumstantial evidence that somebody else was in the house, but it is something I can use. Now we need to figure out what to do with the locked basement door. Do you know if the owners locked it before they left for Vienna?"

Rachele's reaction to the hole in his trousers' pocket had a positive effect on Dario. He was not panicking any more.

"I have to do a check on the entire house once a day. I have to go through all the rooms. I am not supposed to look at the basement. There shouldn't be anything worth taking in there, but I have been down there a few times and I am pretty sure I can describe what I saw with a good level of accuracy."

Rachele wrote something

"What is supposed to be in the basement? Who could give us permission to open the door?"

"Gino Moras or the owner, Laszlo Kron."

"I'd rather not ask Gino Moras. Do you know how to reach Laszlo Kron?"

Rachele could see that Dario had stopped feeling positive.

"Unfortunately not. I am only supposed to deal with Gino Moras."

Rachele thought about it. Then she had an idea.

"It is a long shot, but I wonder whether the Hotel Excelsior has his details."

Dario's face lit up.

"I think so. I think he was a client of the Hotel before he bought the Villa."

Rachele wondered if she had another way to get Mr Kron's details, but she kept it to herself. She told Dario she would ask Mr Dolfin for Mr Kron's contact detail to write asking permission to use a locksmith to open the door to the basement.

When Rachele was back in her office, she called her aunt before she started working on a contract. She was available. She kept the social side as brief as her manners allowed her, then came straight to the point of her call.

"Aunt Deborah, by any chance, do you have a client called Laszlo Kron?"

Countess Pesaro De Bonfili was an art broker; many used her services to be the 'anonymous buyer' or, more often, the 'anonymous seller'. Therefore, she was reluctant to disclose any detail of her clients.

"Is it tied to Mario Dolfin's visit to your law firm before Yom Kippur?"

Rachele knew the countess had those details. Saying she didn't have them would have ended the conversation.

"Yes, without getting into details, I need to ask his permission to call a locksmith to open a basement door."

"Did you know one of Viktor's cousins used to own what is now 'Villa Kalman'? When he passed away, his children sold the house. Mario Dolfin found out before they put it on the market and told Laszlo Kron. I have helped him find some of the painting in his home; nothing a museum would bid for, but a lot of valuable paintings, mostly landscapes. Let me look at my diary."

After a few minutes, the countess gave Rachele her client's address. She also added his Italian was very poor. Mario Dolfin and one of the Hotel Excelsior's receptionist acted as interpreters. Rachele reminded her she was fluent in German and she would write to him in German.

Chapter Four

October 1925

12 October 1925

Rachele did not expect the reply she had from Laszlo Kron. It was a kind but firm letter. He understood Dario Zago's predicament and was concerned about who else could have been coming and going from the Villa. The surprise came when he agreed to Rachele calling a locksmith but also told her he would rather she waited until he was in Venice. He had organised tickets on the night train and would arrive in Venice on Wednesday 14th, in the morning. He did not want to create problems, so he had booked a room at the Excelsior until Sunday.

Rachele was talking to her boss in the office kitchen. Franco Venier shared her surprise at Mr Kron's reaction.

"He is coming rather than telling Gino Moras to sort out the locksmith. By the way, has Mario Dolfin mentioned anything more about us becoming Hotel Excelsior's legal advisors?"

Rachele was busy not drinking her coffee. She found it almost funny that her pregnancy made her stomach dislike coffee. After all, her father ran the largest coffee trading business in the Mediterranean.

"I think he liked he could communicate with me in German. I spoke to Mario Dolfin this morning asking him to recommend a local locksmith, but he did not mention his search for a new legal advisor."

Franco Venier noticed Rachele was not drinking coffee.

"Changing the subject to something more personal. I just noticed you let the coffee grow cold. Is everything all right?"

It was time to tell her boss about her pregnancy. Rachele was nervous but managed a smile.

"As a matter of fact, everything is more than all right. I am expecting. The baby is due in February, more or less around Emma's second birthday."

Franco Venier was not old enough to be her father, but his role in the firm made him speak with a fatherly voice.

"How do you feel? Can you repeat what happened with Emma and let me know if you think you will take a case till its end before you start working on it?"

Rachele was relieved that her boss took the news of her pregnancy so well.

"If Emma is anything to go by, I think I'll continue working until mid-January. I won't take any new case from December. Back to business. Kron has organised an appointment here for Wednesday afternoon. He asked Mario Dolfin to ask Dario if he can be here as well. We have organised the locksmith for the following day."

Franco Venier followed Rachele's lead and was back to business.

"My advice is to organise an independent witness. Don't call the police until you know what is in there. Tell them you waited because you did not want to waste their time."

. . .

14 October 1926

Rachele had no expectation of Laszlo Kron. She did not know who he was and Mario Dolfin and Dario Zago could give her only vague information. She wondered how he had made his money and how come a Hungarian still lived in Vienna. According to her father, Baron Davide Modiano of Trieste, all his Hungarian contacts had moved to Budapest following the end of the Austrian Empire. She had organised the large meeting room, the one almost overlooking Rialto Bridge. When she joined her visitors, she did not expect to see somebody who had the look and the demeanour of her father. She made a mental note to ring his parents to check if they knew him. Rachele introduced herself. Mr Kron waited to sit down until she had sat down. Old-world manners. He came to the point in German.

"Thank you for seeing me. I have asked for Mario Dolfin to be here as a favour. My Italian is not good enough. I also asked Dario to be here because I hoped to show him I trust him, and I am sure nothing of what happened is his fault."

Rachele translated for the benefit of Dario, who relaxed after the introduction. She explained what happened a month earlier and why she thought they would find the evidence that somebody else had been in the Villa in the basement and therefore Dario Zago could not have shot the teenagers.

"Why did you contact me? Gino Moras would have been enough."

Rachele did not want to badmouth the administrator of Kron's Italian estate, so she said she thought she would create fewer problems asking the owner. They agreed to meet at the Lido the following day at 3pm, when the locksmith would open the door to the basement. Laszlo Kron's closing remark surprised her.

"Can you please sort out the paperwork I need to sign to become your client? I will sign the paperwork in Italian provided you have a German translation by Friday morning. You can also bill me for this meeting."

Rachele noticed that Mario Dolfin was not surprised. Maybe it was a good omen for his decision for the future legal advisor of the Hotel Excelsior.

~

Rachele needed to understand Laszlo Kron better. She noticed his address was the same as the Modiano family residence in Vienna. So, she called her father on the odd chance he could give her more information about her new client.

Baron Davide Modiano picked up the call almost immediately. They exchanged the latest family news, then she came to the reason for her call.

"When was the last time you were in Vienna?"

"Your mother and I were there last May. Why?"

"I may have signed up a client, a Mr Laszlo Kron, who lives at your address in apartment 8. Do you know him?"

"I don't, but Michele spends more time in Vienna than we do. He left early. Can you call him tomorrow morning? I am sure he will take your call after dinner if it is urgent."

Rachele hoped her brother would be more useful.

"It is not urgent. Tomorrow is fine."

She closed the conversation as fast as her manners allowed. She hung up, stared at the phone and realised her honorary aunt was another potential source of information. Deborah Camerini, Countess Pesaro De Bonfili, sounded in a good mood when she picked up the phone.

33

"Rachele, how nice to hear from you! Is it a long call? A client is supposed to ring me in about an hour."

"Aunt Deborah, the question is quick. The answer may not be. What can you tell me about Laszlo Kron?"

"You mean the one who owns the villa where Mario Dolfin protégé lives?"

"Yes, Mr Kron is in Venice for a few days and he asked me to prepare the paperwork because he wants to retain me as his lawyer in Venice."

By now, Rachele had been in Deborah Camerini's study so often that she could visualise the furniture. She wondered what kept her aunt. She could hear a door closing. Less than thirty seconds later, her honorary aunt was back on the phone.

"Laszlo Kron retained me to find all the paintings hanging in the Villa and some for his home in Vienna. I even found some antique piece of furniture for him. If you ever see one of the reception rooms, you may think the house has been in his family forever, in reality he bought it from the estate of one of Viktor's cousins about two and a half year ago, in the Spring of 1923."

"Do you know what he does, and how he made his money?"

Rachele could hear the countess laugh.

"If he has retained you as his client, you should not be concerned about the bills. He is the most successful impresario in Vienna, owns three theatres and made a lot of money with Operettas. Laszlo Kron funded the translation and the first performances of 'The Czarda Princess' by Kalman and bought the house with the money he made when the Operetta opened in one of his theatres after the war. He wrote a cheque to Victor's cousin's children for the entire amount as if he were paying a grocery bill."

"Thank you. You have been very helpful."

"How long is he in Venice for? He could be interested in a painting a client wants me to sell."

"He is here until Sunday, but you did not hear it from me."

To end the conversation, Rachele told her aunt she had a couple of things to finish before Gabriele arrived to walk home together. The Countess had not finished yet.

"Do you and Gabriele go out to dinner these days?"

Rachele sensed one of Deborah Camerini's cunning plans.

"Yes, we do. We try to organise things in advance, so we can ask Anita if she minds being at home with Emma. It is a formality, but I'd like to show that I am not taking her for granted."

"Great, I want to invite your brother-in-law, Emanuele, and the daughter of friends of Viktor's. I'd rather not have a repeat of what happened when I invited you and Gabriele for dinner, so I am inviting you two. You are married. You won't give me any surprise."

Rachele did not comment on her honorary aunt's last sentence. She asked her to let her know the date as soon as possible, ended the conversation, shook her head, and thought she had something to share with Gabriele on their way home.

An hour later, Gabriele knocked at her doorpost to ask her if she was ready to go. Rachele collected her coat and briefcase. On their way out, they saw Franco Venier, who congratulated Gabriele for the pregnancy.

Rachele told her husband about her conversation with their

aunt as they were walking down the stairs; Gabriele kissed his wife on the cheek, highly unusual for him.

"She might have forgiven us for scuttling her matchmaking plans, but she has not forgotten."

Countess Pesaro De Bonfili had invited both of them to a Friday night dinner as prospective matches for her son and the daughter of a family friend. They looked at each other and fell in love. Now the countess tells everybody that they were her most successful match. Back then, she had to revise her plan for a future daughter-in-law but did not need a new plan for a wife for one of her honorary nephews.

They crossed the Rialto bridge and took a longer route home. Gabriele wanted to walk past a shop near Rialto where he hoped to find a present for his sister's birthday. When they walked past the empty fish market, they met Sofia, the wife of Gabriele's oldest and closest friend, Paolo Mondani, with Arrigo, their seven-year-old son.

"You saved me a phone call. Paolo has a date for his graduation. I want to organise a dinner."

Meanwhile, Arrigo had grabbed Gabriele, his honorary uncle, and demanded his attention. It was up to Rachele to react.

"That is wonderful news. Please talk to Fiamma. I am sure she will want to be included in the dinner's organisation."

Arrigo had dragged Gabriele to a nearby shop window. Sofia and Rachele looked at them and smiled at each other before Rachele continued.

"By the way, you also have to tell Fiamma and Samuele Paolo's graduation date. I am sure they will want to be there. We will definitely be there."

Arrigo and Gabriele had joined them. Gabriele gestured to his honorary nephew to be quiet in a conspiratorial way. Sofia looked at them, shook her head, and then turned to Rachele.

"Grandma Fiamma has already offered to take care of Arrigo for a few days if we want to go somewhere to celebrate Paolo's graduation."

Chapter Five

October 1925

15 October 1925

Anita had been working for Rachele and Gabriele since January 1922. Over time, she and Rachele had developed a close friendship which made her feel she was part of the family rather than a paid employee. Usually, she was the first one to wake up in the Modiano Mendes household. That morning, when she walked into the kitchen, she saw Rachele cleaning the table after a baking session, a sign that her employer had been anxious about something.

"Good morning, Rachele. Are you in court today or are you not feeling well?"

Rachele had not heard Anita, so she stopped cleaning the table for a few seconds.

"It could be the pregnancy. Today I officially sign my first foreign client. He has not specifically chosen me, but his Italian is not very good and I am the only one fluent in German."

Anita and Rachele could be in the kitchen together, have a conversation, and be busy doing what they had to do, a clear sign of their familiarity. Anita was laying the table for breakfast and making sure that Emma's high chair was clean.

"And that made you bake early in the morning?"

Rachele had now finished cleaning the table and had moved to the sink to wash the utensils she had just used.

"I woke up very early this morning wondering if I have to tell him about my pregnancy and whether he will change his mind about retaining our firm."

Anita started preparing coffee and a hot chocolate for Rachele.

"As much as I love the results of your morning anxiety, I think you have no reason to be anxious."

A smell of freshly baked Kipferl[1] was coming out of the oven. Anita was the one nearer the stove, so she checked the biscuits. They both heard Gabriele walk into the kitchen talking to Emma. He put her down in her high chair.

"Good morning Anita. Rachele, I could smell the biscuits from Emma's bedroom are you all right?"

Anita looked at Rachele with her best reassuring face. Rachele kissed Emma on the forehead.

"I think being pregnant turned a normal concern into anxiety. Anyway, I am sure you will enjoy the products of my anxiety. The Kipferl will be ready before we have to leave!"

Rachele was reviewing her translation into German of the firm's paperwork for new clients when Franco Venier knocked on the doorpost. He sat down with a huge grin on his face.

"I just finished a phone call with Mario Dolfin. Our law firm is one of the two leading candidates to be their new legal advisor. They want you as their leading counsel."

Rachele's reaction surprised him.

"Not another one!"

Rachele quickly regrouped.

"I am thrilled that they may sign and that they want me. I am just very anxious that I can do the job they deserve now that I am pregnant."

Franco Venier hoped to sound reassuring and dismissive of her fears at the same time.

"I am not. I have lined up an excellent substitute for you when you have the baby."

"Who is it?"

Franco Venier had a huge grin on his face

"Me! They have asked for more information. Please remember to drop by the Hotel Excelsior before you meet Mr Kron and the locksmith. Give Mario Dolfin the paperwork. Please remember to wear your 'sales face' when you deal with him. We are not their legal advisors yet."

Then he stood up and left the office. Rachele could only think of how lucky she was that she had found such a supportive employer. She had come across a lot of women who were forced to give up work the moment they announced they were pregnant.

A phone call interrupted her musing. Since she had not called her brother yet, he called her. Michele Modiano had little to add about Laszlo Kron, but calmed down her fears reminding her that their eldest sister Greta, the surgeon, was back in the operating room about one month after giving birth to each one of her three children, and she did not have Rachele's secret weapon, Anita.

❧

On her way to the Lido, Rachele felt queasy after she boarded the waterbus. She had to sit inside. It never happened when she was expecting Emma. She wondered whether her current pregnancy would be more difficult. By the time the waterbus docked at the Lido, she had talked herself into not being her own prophet of doom.

She was early enough to have the time to walk to the Hotel Excelsior and have a brief conversation with Mario Dolfin. It was a long walk from the *vaporetto*[2] stop, and Rachele did not take the shortest route. She wanted to walk by the beach. Walking alongside *Lungomare Malamocco*[3] cleared her head. She looked at the empty beach and thought of Emma. It was her turn to give her a bath and put her to bed. She was looking forward to her time with her daughter and wondered whether her stomach could cope with a ride on a speedboat if things took longer than expected.

When she reached the Hotel, the receptionist directed her to the terrace. Mario Dolfin was sitting at one of the tables. He stood up and invited Rachele to sit with him.

"Before we start with our business, I know how long we have. Dario Zago has asked me to go along as an independent witness."

Rachele sat down and put her briefcase on a nearby chair.

"Dario Zago will become a smart lawyer."

A waiter approached her, asking if she wanted anything to drink. Rachele ordered a light lemonade, with more water than pressed lemon. She thought she had better be on the safe side. They talked about how pleasant it was to sit in the sun on a nice October day. Mario Dolfin waited until the waiter brought the lemonade, then gave her a folder. She gave him the paperwork and started looking at the folder's content while she was sipping her drink.

"As you know, I requested you as our lead advisor. You are fluent in German, you speak French, in the event we have a problem with one of our guests, your language skills will be very useful. There is a separate note on top of the paperwork detailing all the services available to you and your family for free or at a discounted rate if we chose your firm."

Rachele looked at the list. She felt she had to disclose her pregnancy.

"Thank you and thank you for the privileges. We shall most definitely use the beach next summer. I have to inform you I am pregnant. The baby is due in February next year. I plan to do what I did with Emma, my daughter, and come back to work towards the end of April. Franco Venier will replace me from mid-January, or earlier, depending on how I feel, until I come back to work full time in May."

Mario Dolfin pointed out that the privileges listed for her will also be available to two other named lawyer from the same law firm. He also offered the use of one of the hotel speedboats to go back to Venice when they had finished at Villa Kalman.

When they arrived at Villa Kalman, Rachele left Mario Dolfin with Dario Zago to wait for the locksmith. She and Laszlo Kron went to his study. He had to sign some paperwork.

"For any future conversations with the police; it is important to establish that I am here as your and Dario Zago's legal advisor at the time they opened the door of the basement.

Mario Dolfin is here as an independent witness. He hasn't signed the paperwork to be a client of the Venier-Zanin law firm yet."

Laszlo Kron started reading the German text. Rachele took another document out of her briefcase.

"This is an affidavit I translated the Italian text into German and an independent translator verified it. The other document is a letter signed by Franco Venier, one of the two partners, stating in German and Italian that the law firm will be bound by the German text."

Mr Kron signed the paperwork.

"I will be back in Venice next month. I have negotiations with two Italian theatres and with an impresario that wants a new translation of the Czardas princess in Italian. If the negotiations turn into something concrete, I will need your advice."

Rachele countersigned the relevant bit of the paperwork and was putting everything in her briefcase when Dario Zago knocked at the door to tell them that the locksmith had arrived. They moved downstairs to the basement door. The general agreement was that they would look at what was in the basement once the locksmith had changed the locks. Fifteen minutes later, the locksmith had finished and was putting away his tools. Rachele turned to Mr Kron in German.

"Patience. Wait until the locksmith has gone."

Mr Kron looked at her, remove his hands from the door handle.

"If you say so."

Once the locksmith had left, Mr Kron opened the door and turned the light on. The steps they could see reached only to a landing. A rifle leant against the wall on a corner of the landing. Dario Zago saw it first. He turned to Rachele.

"I think we should not touch it. There might be evidence that leads to the identity of the shooter and clear my name."

Mario Dolfin heard Dario and stopped Mr Kron. Rachele first turned to Dario.

"You are right. We should not proceed any further."

She then turned to Mr Kron.

"It is important we stop here. We must not touch anything else until the police have been here. They may find fingerprints that will help identify the shooter. We need to call them now."

Mr Kron stopped. They all went back into the kitchen and closed the door. Mr Kron locked the door and took all the three keys the locksmith had given him.

"It may be too late today, but if you can, Madam Avvocato Modiano, I would like you to come with me to the police tomorrow around 10.30. Consider it billable time, bring anything I have to sign to approve it. I will inform Gino Moras that he must be there as well. Mario Dolfin will help me if my Italian is not good enough."

Rachele repeated what her client had just said for the benefit of Dario Zago.

"Dario, did the police take your fingerprint?"

Dario was reluctant to admit it, but they had.

"The day after I came to you, when they said they suspected me of attempted murder and I should not leave the Lido under any circumstance."

"Great, so they might even exclude you as soon as they have retrieved the rifle."

Mario Dolfin had been discussing something with Mr Kron. He then turned to Rachele.

"It doesn't look like there is anything else we have to do here. The Hotel speedboat will be ready to take you back to Venice whenever you like. Mr Kron has asked me to send the speedboat tomorrow morning to take you to the Lido. Let the driver know where to pick you up."

~

Rachele had to wait for one of the hotel speedboats to be back. Mario Dolfin suggested something to eat. A full stomach would do better on the journey back to Venice. Later, she was relieved to notice the dry biscuits worked. The driver dropped her a few steps from home, by the Ruga Bella bridge. They agreed to meet by Rialto bridge, near her office, the following morning.

Rachele was in a good mood as she was climbing the two flights of steps. If Gabriele did not have to work late, they would have time for one of their walks. She was looking forward to a romantic evening walk with her husband. Anita heard that somebody opened the front door and appeared in the hall, followed by Emma, who toddled towards her mother, expecting to be picked up. Anita intercepted her, picked her up, kissed her on the cheek and passed her on to Rachele.

"I did not expect you back so early. I am halfway through cleaning her bath. The water is boiling. You have around forty minutes before everything is ready."

Anita knew Rachele was listening to her, even though she was also trying to take her jacket off and pay attention to Emma.

"Wonderful, I have time to call the office and tell the secretary that I have to go back to the Lido tomorrow morning."

Despite Anita's protestation, she picked up Emma and went to her study, telling her daughter she had to be quiet because mummy had to work before her bath.

Rachele loved the time she spent giving her daughter a bath and putting her to bed. Once her daughter was settled and asleep, she went back to the laundry room and found Gabriele sorting out the mess.

"I was about to do it now."

Gabriele turned around, smiled and kissed his wife.

"You know that Anita and I will not let you empty the bowl you used to give Emma a bath. It is too heavy. Once I emptied it, I thought that if I clean the mess, we may have time for a walk before dinner. What about walking to Rialto, have a drink and come back?"

Rachele started picking up and folding the towels she used and the clothes Emma was wearing.

"Do we have time? Let's check with Anita once this room is presentable. If we don't, we might just walk to San Stae church, look at the Grand Canal, and come back."

Rachele loved being around her husband. The two of them sorted out the laundry, checked with Anita, then left for their walk and a drink near the Rialto bridge.

16 October 1925

Rachele did not want to be late for Shabbat[4]; beyond any religious observance, it was family time. She loved her job and was prepared to work at any hour, provided she could have time for her daughter and her husband. Shabbat was the time for her and Gabriele to be a family, either alone or with other family members. A time when they put on hold all their professional concerns until sunset on Saturday, or, if they were not urgent, until Sunday lunchtime. She and Gabriele were determined not to discuss anything connected with work on Shabbat. However, Shabbat required preparation and Rachele contributed to the preparations of the extended Mendes clan. That week she couldn't. It was only after Anita said she had to do what she had to do that Rachele stopped feeling guilty.

At 9.30, she was at the jetty near Rialto bridge waiting for the Hotel Excelsior speedboat. About an hour later, she was inside the police station with Mr Kron and Dario Zago. Mr Kron had decided not to speak a word of Italian. He had already agreed on the tactic with Rachele. When Gino Moras arrived, Laszlo Kron introduced him to Rachele and Dario Zago. Rachele explained to him why Mr Kron has requested his presence. She also pointed out that now she was also Mr Kron's legal advisor. When the agent at reception told them that the Vice-Commissario was ready to see them, they all walked in. Mr Kron explained in halting Italian that he had instructed his lawyer, Rachele Modiano Mendes, to explain the situation, because she could do better than him.

Rachele summarised what happened when they called a locksmith and open the door to the basement. Once the locksmith had changed the locks, they walked in, turned the light on, and saw the rifle. At that moment, Rachele suggested they all walk back and close the door in order not to contaminate the scene. Dario Zago was leading the group, and he stopped when he saw the rifle. He was on the third step. The group also included Mr Kron and Mario Dolfin, the manager of Hotel Excelsior, who had agreed to be there as an independent witness. Mr Kron had followed her legal advice and did not use his set of keys to open the door, but waited for the locksmith to change the lock. Once they had established that somebody else other than Dario Zago had access to the lower ground floor, they wanted to keep any evidence as intact as possible. Mr Kron also wanted to make sure that nobody could have unauthorised access, hence why he had called a locksmith to change the locks of the door leading to the basement.

The Vice-Commissario turned to Gino Moras.

"And who are you, and why are you here?"

Gino Moras started speaking with a very confident tone of voice.

"I am Gino Moras, Mr Kron's accountant for his Italian business. Before he had organised somebody to stay in the house when he was not in Venice, he had left me a set of keys with instructions to check the mail and take care of anything that happened while he was in Vienna."

Rachele noticed that Gino's voice was growing less and less steady. He sounded more and more nervous. She was sure he was hiding something. The Vice-Commissario continued asking questions.

"If you had a set of keys, would you think that whoever had access to the basement took them from you, or did Mr Zago have that key as well?"

Dario felt it was his turn to say something.

"After Mario Dolfin discussed with me the idea of staying at Villa Kalman as a caretaker while Mr Kron was not in Venice, we went to Gino Moras to organise copies of six keys: front gate, back gate, the two keys for the front door, the key for the back door and the key to the attic just in case somebody had to access the roof. I never had the key to the basement."

Rachele continued to be impressed by Dario Zago, she decided to talk to her boss about him. She also noticed that Gino Moras was getting more and more nervous. The policeman turned to Gino Moras.

"That only leaves you,"

"I have been thinking about that since last night. A month ago I was tiding up the drawer where I keep spare sets of keys. I do not just have Mr Kron's keys. I manage a few properties that are rented out in the summer, so I have several sets of keys. They all have a label with the address on the key ring.

Anyway, my wife called me home early. We had a problem with a leaking tap in the bathroom. So I left in a hurry and forgot the keys on my desk. Somebody could have walked into my office, retrieved Villa Kalman's set of keys and copied them."

Rachele was sure that the Vice Commissario also noticed Gino Moras's unease. She felt she had to say something if they could leave the Police station at an acceptable time.

"I am not Gino Moras's legal representative. But, I would like to point out that at the moment you have no reason not to believe him. I suggest you send agents to retrieve the rifle and dust it for fingerprints. Once you have the identity of the shooter, you can talk to Mr Moras, if it is still relevant."

The Vice Commissario looked at Rachele as if she were from outer space. It wasn't the first time somebody had underestimated her. As a female lawyer, she was used to establishing her credibility with strangers. He agreed with Rachele, but told Gino Moras not to leave the Lido without telling the police where he was going. He would let Dario Zago know when he could send a team at Villa Kalman and dismissed everybody.

Gino Moras asked Rachele if he could see her as soon as possible. Rachele gave him her business card.

"Ring the office on Monday and ask them to find the nearest slot. Tell them it is urgent and they will check with me before arranging an appointment."

Gino Moras took the card and left. Dario Zago told them he would like to go back to the Villa. He was hoping to study for a few more hours that day. Mr Kron invited him to dinner at Hotel Excelsior. On the way, he and Rachele were discussing their perceptions of their visit to the police station in German, thinking Dario Zago would not understand.

"Mr Kron, I think Gino Moras is hiding something. I think he needs legal advice, but I promise you I shall take his case only if I am hundred per cent sure there is no conflict of interest. When are you going back?"

They had entered the hotel. Before going to the concierge's desk, Mr Kron stopped.

"I am going back on Sunday and will be in touch from Vienna after you have met Gino Moras. I am thinking of replacing him, but I won't decide until after you have spoken to him."

Then they approached the concierge where Mr Kron asked them to make sure there was a speedboat available to take Rachele home.

Chapter Six

October-November 1925

19 October 1925

Rachele had divided her Monday morning between a contract and the notes she had from the previous week. She was confident that the fingerprints on the rifle would clear Dario Zago. Franco Venier had agreed to talk to him. Her introductory comment that the 'young man had a strong sense of evidence and what he had to do not to compromise it' convinced her boss.

She was putting things away before going home for lunch when Alvise Cantoni appeared at her door. Alvise had been a friend of Gabriele from primary school and had joined the law firm a year after Rachele did, working for the other partner, Giovanni Zanin. Alvise had something confidential to discuss. He spoke with a low voice, slightly above whispering.

"I am not inviting myself to lunch. I have something to discuss with you and it is better if we do it outside this office, so we are Rachele and Alvise rather than two practicing lawyers. Do you mind if I walk home with you and Gabriele?"

Rachele closed the drawer where she had just put the contract she was working on and lifted her head.

"I am sure if I call Anita in advance, lunch would not be a problem, but you obviously know that Gabriele will hear whatever we discuss on the way home."

Alvise leant on one of the chairs.

"Gabriele should not be surprised to hear what I want to discuss with you. It follows a conversation I had with him a while ago as we were walking from synagogue to your in-law's home for dinner after a Friday night service."

20 October 1925

It was a crisp Autumn Day, unusually clear and sunny at a time of the year when clouds and fog were the norm. Gabriele and Rachele were walking to work along what they called the scenic route rather than the shortest route. They were holding hands, their height difference made lower by Rachele's heels. They were silent for the first ten minutes of their walk, just enjoying the closeness. When they were about to walk past the Mondani's home, they noticed Paolo walking Arrigo to school. They waved. Paolo waved back; Arrigo shouted "Good morning Uncle Gabriele and Aunt Rachele." Gabriele and Rachele could hear Paolo telling him to keep a street voice, waving would have been enough.

"Arrigo is playing the honorary big brother with Emma very well. We should organise a lunch with Paolo and Sofia so they can bring Arrigo with them. We should also have Alvise and Viola with Franco, another honorary brother."

Rachele tightened her grip on Gabriele's arm, looked around, and spoke in a tone of voice barely above a whisper. She did not want other passers-by to hear her.

"How long have you known that Alvise is a sympathiser of the Social Democracy party[1]?"

His wife's question surprised Gabriele. He tried to stop, but Rachele pushed him a bit. A silent message that they should be moving.

"You know, I dislike talking about politics. My job means I am above political parties, at least here in Venice. One Friday night before Rosh Hashanah[2] we were walking to my parents from synagogue and I was discussing how I feel strongly that my job stops me from getting any party membership card even though they put pressure on us to join the Fascist Party."

"You never told me they are putting pressure on you to join the Fascist Party."

"I did not think it was important enough to bring it up. Alvise told me he agreed with my mindset. He never officially joined the Social Democracy party for similar reasons, although his job differs from mine. He is attending a lot of their events and knows many people."

They had reached the top of the Rialto bridge and Rachele stopped for what she called her "Canaletto moment" looking at the Grand Canal for a few minutes.

Gino Moras was standing when Rachele walked into the meeting room. Rachele could see he was nervous. She felt she had to warn him before he mentioned anything compromising.

"Good afternoon, Mr Moras. Before we start, I have to point out that I am Mr Zago and Mr Kron's legal representative and I have to protect their interests. At the moment, I am not bound to keep anything you say confidential, especially if it helps my clients. If you are seeking independent legal advice, I may have to suggest a different lawyer in the law firm."

Gino Moras sat down. He looked nervous but determined.

"I do not think there is anything confidential in what I have to say, or at least not in what I want to disclose at the beginning. I'll leave it to you to figure out if you need another lawyer present afterwards."

Rachele sat down with a notepad.

"You understand I had to say that."

"I do, and I am sure that what I want to share now will not damage your clients. You may not know, but three weeks ago, the black shirts raided the Venetian headquarters of the Socialist party and beat up some members they found inside."

"I did not know that."

"Well, my brother was one of those that got beaten up. Anyway, they needed another place to meet. My brother knows I manage properties that are rented out in the summer and empty most of the time between October and May."

Rachele felt she knew what was coming but had to keep the appearance of conjecture.

"And you think your brother took the set of keys from your desk and had that duplicated?"

Gino Moras took a deep breath. He was relieved it was in the open.

"Yes, I wondered if it was him who shot at the two boys."

"Thank you for using verbs that do not make me think that you have actual knowledge your brother 'borrowed' the set of keys and, later, he shot at the boys. I think a colleague can better advise you. Let me see who is available."

Rachele did not volunteer that she and Alvise had agreed he would step in the moment Gino Moras asked for legal advice. She excused herself and promised to be back with a colleague. Ten minutes later, she was back.

"My colleague, Avvocato Cantoni, will be with you in fifteen minutes. He is closing another meeting. Meanwhile, a secretary will come to sort out coffee, tea, or other type of refreshment. It was a pleasure to meet you. Thank you for coming."

Rachele went back to her office to write a letter to Mr Kron. She summarised what she felt she could share about her meeting with Gino Moras and said that, in her opinion, he should not be fired, or at least not yet.

27 October 1925

It was Rachele's turn to give Emma her breakfast. She found herself alone in bed. Gabriele had got up without waking her up. After she got dressed, she put on an overall covering her 'work clothes', took Emma out of bed and walked into the kitchen holding her. Gabriele was not there, only Anita.

She heard the front door right after she placed Emma in her highchair, ready to start the 'battle for breakfast'. Gabriele entered the kitchen carrying the paper.

"A couple of days ago you mentioned you wanted to start reading the paper every day even though you were not interested in politics, so this morning when I woke up I looked at the clock by my bedside and decided I could go out and buy the newspaper. The newsagent is not very far."

He approached the table and kissed Rachele, then Emma. Rachele kept watching Emma's attempt to feed herself.

"Thank you. I still dislike politics, but I feel I need to read about it now, given what is going on."

Later, on their way to work, Gabriele asked Rachele what made her decide to read the paper every day. Rachele tried to answer without revealing details of a potential case.

"Last week somebody tied a development in a case to an event that involved the black shirts and members of the

Socialist party. I realised I did not know that these things were happening. I need to be better informed."

9 November 1925

Rachele rarely believed in fate. However, sometimes strange coincidences happened. She had not heard from Laszlo Kron for a couple of weeks. She was waiting for two theatres to send her contracts for permission to change the script of Operettas for which Mr Kron held all the rights. A letter from him arrived the same day as one contract. It was also the day she was going to introduce Dario Zago to her boss. The letter announced he would arrive in Venice in a month because he had business in Italy. His family would follow ten days later, once the schools in Vienna closed for Christmas. They were going to spend Christmas and New Year in Venice. He asked her to organise a meeting on December 10th.

She was writing a note for the secretary who managed everybody's diaries when the receptionist told her Dario Zago had arrived. Rachele left her office to greet him and take him to the kitchen for coffee before meeting Franco Venier. Dario was excited. The police had told him the fingerprints were most definitely not his. He was not the shooter and was free to leave the Lido whenever he wanted.

Rachele congratulated him and took him to her boss.

Back at her desk, she took out the contract from the envelope, but there was something nagging her. She needed somebody else's opinion. Five minutes later, Alvise was in her office.

"How can I help you?"

"I have an interesting issue. I think I know something that might interest the police, but it is just me adding two and two, and, with no evidence, might end up with twenty-six instead of four."

"If there is no watertight evidence, you have no obligation to inform them. Are you protecting a client?"

"Not exactly. I may protect one of your clients."

Alvise changed his posture. He sat straight, almost waiting for a punch.

"Tell me more."

"Last week Mussolini disbanded the Socialist Party. Last Saturday, he arrested leaders of the opposition. Do you remember Gino Moras? Is he your client?"

"He is. What about him?"

"He told me he thought his brother took the keys when he left them on the table to go home to lunch. Dario Zago told me they have ruled him out as the shooter of the two teenagers. I wonder if Gino Moras's brother was the shooter."

Alvise stood up and started pacing the room.

"Do you have any evidence?"

"No, the police have not identified the owner of the fingerprints they lifted from the rifle's handle."

Alvise sat, he was now more relaxed.

"This is an opinion, you would not be considered a reliable witness in court. I think you should keep quiet."

Rachele stood, walked around the desk, and sat next to Alvise. She lowered her voice.

"Were you in any way affected by what happened last week?"

Alvise smiled nervously, almost laughed.

"No, I was not. As you know, I am not a card-carrying member of an opposition party, just a sympathiser. There is no way I can be elected as one of their leaders."

Later, Franco Venier made a quick stop in her office to tell her she was right. Dario Zago had the potential to become an excellent lawyer. He will stay in touch, maybe offer him occasional work as a researcher.

When she was walking home with Gabriele at the end of her day, Rachele had the odd feeling she had not heard the last of Gino Moras. Gabriele was used to her being silent as they were walking home. The way she was holding his arm meant she was still thinking of work. When they arrived home, her face lit up when Emma ran towards them, with Anita behind her.

Chapter Seven

December 1925

4 December 1925

Gabriele, Rachele, Gabriele's brother Emanuele, and Count Pesaro De Bonfili were walking to the Pesaro De Bonfili residence after Friday night service. Gabriele was talking to his honorary uncle about the changes in the atmosphere at work, almost a month after Mussolini had ordered the arrest of the opposition leaders. Rachele and Emanuele were walking behind them.

"Emanuele, relax! Don't look like somebody about to be hanged. You may meet your future wife this evening."

Emanuele looked as if an alarm clock had just jolted him from a deep sleep.

"The 'future wife' does not worry me. I am worried I might have to spend the evening pretending to be interested in a plain and boring young woman who, in Aunt Deborah's eyes, deserves a husband."

Rachele's laughter made Gabriele turn back for a moment. She was sure he would ask her why she laughed so loud as soon as they had a moment together.

"Aunt Deborah has taste. Gabriele and I met during one of her Friday night dinners!"

"Yes, and she had planned two matches. You and my brother falling in love at first sight was not in her plans."

Rachele changed tactic, teasing obviously did not work.

"I am not sure I can put a face to the name of the young woman she has invited to dinner, but I am sure your honorary aunt only wants the best for you. She had lined up a very interesting person for Gabriele. Ironically, Viola is now married to Alvise Cantoni, one of two Gabriele's closest and oldest friends."

Rachele failed to change her brother-in-law's expectation of a boring evening.

"Let's put it this way. I accepted the invitation to get my mother and aunt Deborah off my back. After tonight, I'll be able to tell them they tried, but I'll find my wife."

Gabriele and Rachele were walking home after dinner. It was a clear night. They were taking a long walk home, enjoying the atmosphere of the night and each other's company. Gabriele wanted a 'Canaletto moment' with a full moon. They were talking about their memory of the first time they met, when they approached Rialto bridge. Rachele changed the subject and started discussing the dinner that had just happened.

"Do you think Aunt Deborah did it again?"

They were walking arm in arm, Gabriele put his right hand in his trousers pocket as an indirect way to draw his wife closer.

"Only time will tell. Emanuele may have offered to walk

home the young lady he met a few hours ago just to be polite."

They had now reached the top of Rialto Bridge, they stopped to look at the Canal Grande and the moon.

"Somehow I do not think so. Emanuele was nervous, and a bit annoyed before dinner. He did not seem annoyed by the time dinner ended."

They started walking again. Once they crossed the bridge, Gabriele put his right arm around his wife's shoulder.

"Do you think history is repeating itself?"

Rachele stopped walking, took her husband's arm away from her shoulder and looked at him, acting as if she were annoyed but smiling.

"History? May I remind you it happened about five years ago?"

"You are right, and aunt Deborah was not thinking of introducing me to you."

"That as well."

Rachele put her arm around her husband. They walked the rest of the way home in silence, enjoying their closeness. Gabriele thought it may have been less than five years, but he was still in seventh heaven just walking next to his wife.

10 December 1925

Rachele was supervising Emma's attempt to feed herself and was also talking to Anita, who was sorting out breakfast for the grown-ups. They were talking about what they had heard from the family about Friday night dinner.

"Yesterday you helped Fiamma with Shabbat lunch. Did you hear any comments about Emanuele?"

Anita had just put the coffee pot on the stove and was taking out of the oven the cake Rachele had prepared before Emma woke up.

"Fiamma told me that Countess Deborah was thrilled about the way the evening went."

Rachele clapped because Emma had cleared the plate and there was not much on the table or on her bib, a clear sign Emma had eaten most of the food. She made sure that Anita congratulated Emma as well. Once the congratulations were over, she replied to the question Anita did not ask.

"That is a very enigmatic statement. Being 'happy about the way the evening went' may mean that the conversation flowed, which it did, or that everybody liked the food, which we did, or that her matchmaking evening was successful, which is the bit I'd like to know."

"Why don't you ask Emanuele tomorrow night?"

Gabriele chose that moment to appear.

"Ask my brother what?"

Anita and Rachele looked at each other as if they had been plotting something. Gabriele answered his question.

"I see. You are talking about whether aunt Deborah's attempt at matchmaking was successful."

The two women tried to deny it, but Gabriele did not let them get away with it.

When Rachele and Gabriele met Alvise at the café near their office, he asked them about the previous Friday night's dinner. Gabriele almost choked, trying not to laugh while he was drinking his coffee.

"How did you know about the dinner?"

"This is Venice, and we are talking about the Jewish community of Venice. Viola's mother knows Emanuele's young lady's mother, so she knew about the dinner and asked me to ask you how it went."

Gabriele paid for the coffees and kissed his wife. When they were outside, Gabriele had the last word before Alvise and Rachele climbed the two flights of steps to the office.

"Why don't I ask my mother if you, Viola, and Franco can come to lunch on Shabbat? Franco and Emma can play together, and you can ask my brother directly."

Rachele was smiling at the thought of the umpteenth Venetian Jewish mother's conspiracy, and noticed Alvise tried to control his face

"I'll discuss it with Viola at lunch and I'll let Rachele know."

Rachele was reviewing her notes on the contracts she had to check for Laszlo Kron when the receptionist appeared to tell her he was early and asked her whether she was available to meet him now. She was, so she picked her notepad, the two contracts with her notes. And got up to join her client in one of the meeting rooms.

"Welcome to Venice Mr Kron. How was your journey?"

Laszlo Kron was lost in his thoughts and had not heard Rachele come in. He stood up without looking and almost knocked down his briefcase that he had put on the chair next to him. He recovered his manners and bowed to Rachele.

"Good morning Avvocato Modiano. I always find the journey in the night train relaxing. I leave Vienna reading a book, I fall asleep, wake up, have breakfast, and I am in Venice."

"It is a great way to travel. The only downside is that you miss the scenery. I have examined the two contracts you sent me and I have a few points to discuss with you."

The receptionist knocked at the door and came in with the refreshments she had organised. Mr Kron thanked her in Italian. He waited for her to leave the room and then switched back to German.

"There is something else I want to discuss with you. If you think the conversations about the contracts will take too long, we can organise another meeting. Let's start with the contracts.:"

Rachele spent the best part of an hour discussing the contracts. Once her clients had decided which changes he wanted, they were ready to move to whatever else he wanted to discuss with her. Rachele looked at her watch.

"Since you were here half an hour early, I have an extra half an hour. If you think it will take longer, I need to check with the receptionist when my next appointment is."

Laszlo Kron put the notepad where he had written notes about the decisions they had made on the contracts back in his briefcase.

"I think my question won't tale long. I don't know how long your answer will take. Hypothetically, what consequences would I face if I provide indirect help to people who belong to opposition parties here in Italy?"

"The current situation here in Italy is vague. About a month ago, Mussolini disbanded the Socialist party, arrested opposition leaders, membership of the Socialist party is illegal but your ideas are not, or at least not yet. If you help people who were part of any action against the government or planned actions against the government, that would be illegal. Anything else is not illegal yet."

The answer was vague, but Laszlo Kron expected nothing else from his lawyer. Rachele thought of the conversations she had with Alvise and Gino Moras. As Mr Kron's lawyer, she had to give him another advice.

"Mr Kron, I hope you know that, as your lawyer, I can only advise you to respect the laws of the Kingdom of Italy."

"I am well aware of that. I asked to make sure I respect the laws of a country I love."

Rachele did not miss that her client's facial expression did not match the seriousness of his tone of voice.

As she was seeing her client out, Rachele had an idea.

"How long will you be in Venice, Mr Kron?"

"I will stay till January 10th. My family is joining me for Christmas and New Year. We are opening the Villa."

"When will your family join you?"

"They arrive next Friday morning. My children are still in school."

"If you are alone in Venice, would you like to come for lunch on Sunday? There is somebody I would like you to meet. I need to confirm it with my husband first. May I call you this evening?"

"It will be a pleasure. I am staying at the Hotel Excelsior until Tuesday. By then Villa Kalman will be ready for me and my family."

On her way back to her office, Rachele went looking for Alvise. They needed to have a chat outside the office. She needed to run something past him with no professional constraints.

Gabriele and Rachele had developed the perfect routine to go to synagogue on Saturday mornings. Gabriele would go first, Rachele would linger in bed longer, play with Emma and then go to synagogue. Although Anita was not Jewish, she volunteered to help with the meal at Gabriele's parents and would take Emma to synagogue not long before the end of the service. That day was one of the two Shabbats a month when Rachele's mother-in-law, Fiamma, and Countess Deborah would organise lunch for both families. During the synagogue service, she noticed her aunt kept looking at her. Rachele was sure that Countess Pesaro De Bonfili would share with her whatever was in her mind. It happened while they were on their way to lunch, after the service. The countess approached Rachele when they were crossing Campo del Ghetto Novo on their way to Gabriele's parents' home.

"I do not know how to say it tactfully, so I won't try. You are an elegant woman. That dress doesn't suit you."

"I know, but I can only wear maternity dresses these days and they are neither smart nor elegant."

"How far gone are you?"

"I am at the end of the seventh month. The baby is due in February, like Emma."

"How convenient. Do you mind if I talk to my dressmaker to see how quickly she can make you something more appropriate? I hate the idea of your appearing in court wearing that."

Rachele was touched and annoyed at the same time.

"I am not sure it is necessary. My arrangement with my boss means I will not appear in court. I could not stand for the time I might have to stand during a trial, let alone have the energy for it."

Rachele could not talk her aunt out of her mission.

"Well, let me check if we can organise something better to wear. It is a question of dignity."

Rachele knew resistance was futile when the countess was on a self-imposed mission. She thanked her and re-joined her husband.

"What did aunt Deborah want?"

"To turn me into an elegant, expecting mother."

"You are an elegant, expecting mother."

"Maybe in your eyes, the way I see it, she has a point."

Chapter Eight

December 1925

13 December 1925

Lunch had gone better than Rachele expected. She had wondered how Laszlo Kron would fit in a small group of dining companions that had known each other for quite a while. She should not have worried. He entertained the adults with stories from the theatre, using a lot of Italian and only occasionally asking Rachele to help, and played with the toddlers in between courses. As usual, Anita had eaten with them. After lunch, she cleared the meal before going out. Gabriele and Alvise's wife, Viola, were playing with the children and Rachele invited Alvise and Laszlo Kron to follow her into the study. Rachele let the two men sit in the armchairs. She preferred the chair. It was easier to get up. She passed on the biscuits Anita had brought to the study before lunch, asked Alvise to take care of the drinks for him and Mr Kron, then she came to the point.

"Mr Kron, when you asked me your hypothetical question, I realised we had to have an informal conversation. A conversation we had to have in a location where I could forget I was an officer of the court and could deny we ever discussed whatever we were discussing. By the way, Alvise is also forgetting he is an officer of the court."

Mr Kron had figured out that there was an agenda behind the invitation. He congratulated himself for having asked Rachele to be his lawyer in Italy.

"Mrs Modiano, I think we are on similar wavelengths. Before we continue, may I ask why Mr Cantoni has joined us?"

Rachele translated for Alvise, who was ready for that question. When he and Rachele discussed lunch, he expected to have to come clean. The language barrier was slowing things down.

"I have been a friend of Rachele's husband since we were five. When he and Rachele got engaged, he introduced us and we became good friends. We are both lawyers working for the Venier-Zanin law firm. I work for the other partner. Rachele trusts me and she thinks I could be useful. That's why I am here."

Rachele started translating but Laszlo Kron waved a hand, signalling he had understood. Rachele felt the need to add,

"I trust Alvise with my life. Gabriele and I are aware of some aspects of his life that he would not be free to disclose in his role as an officer of the court. I would also add that if I am wrong, we enjoyed your company and I am happy I invited you."

Laszlo Kron asked who baked those Kipferl. They were better than anything he had tasted in Vienna. Rachele thought it was a tactic to buy time, but went along. She demurely replied she had baked them. Laszlo Kron praised her baking skills, ate another Kipferl and asked Rachele to wave a hand when he had to stop to allow her to translate. He took a deep breath.

"You guessed right, but it is a long story. In 1920, I helped people that were not liked by the Bela Kun's government[1]

leave Hungary. It started with me trying to bring my parents to Vienna given the rising antisemitism in Hungary, by the end of the Kun's government my home was the Vienna 'station' for several Hungarian Jews leaving our country. I know Gino Moras was active in one of the opposition parties that the Italian government declared illegal last month. He asked me if I minded whether he used the garden shed to shelter people who were at risk of receiving hostile visits from the Fascist militia. He did not explain why but he told me I could trust you."

Rachele bowed her head thanking her client for the confidence.

"Maybe because, based on what he told me, I suspect his brother shot at those two teenagers a few months ago, but said nothing to the police."

Once Rachele translated what she had just said, Alvise felt the need to come clean.

"I also am a sympathiser of one of those parties who had their leader arrested last month. Which is the real reason I am here."

Rachele felt the need to summarise.

"So, you want to know how to avoid being on the wrong side of the law and still allow your garden shed to be used by unknown guests."

"Exactly."

Alvise had a very concise answer

"Ignore details. Gino Moras has a good reason to have the keys to the Villa: he should not tell you who spends the night in the shed, when somebody spends the night in the shed, etc. I would suggest you put black curtains on the windows in the shed so nobody from the house can see light through the windows."

"That is an excellent point, but I may have to find a way to suggest it to him without doing so."

Rachele got up to retrieve the glasses and the saucers.

"That's right, and if there is nothing else, we may join my husband and Alvise's wife."

Laszlo Kron turned to her.

"We only need to organise a way to communicate outside the law firm."

"Easy. Invite us for coffee. Gabriele is well trained. He can turn blind and deaf if I ask him."

15 December 1925

Rachele loved walking. She loved walking around Venice. After over four years, the pleasure of familiarity had replaced the novelty. However, she was starting her eighth month of pregnancy, so Gabriele decided to try a different route to work. They were on their way to take the waterbus to Rialto. Walking all the way would have been faster and more direct, but Gabriele thought she would enjoy sitting down after a short walk and then have another short walk before going to the office.

They went inside. Once Rachele sat down, she continued the conversation they had started before boarding.

"Emma has eaten all the rice pudding prepared by Anita, without leaving any on the table or the floor."

"It is not the healthiest breakfast. Emma loves it, which might explain her progress in feeding herself. By the way, I enjoyed last Sunday's lunch."

Rachele did not understand the sudden change of subject, but she figured out it was not something he was prepared to discuss in public. Gabriele nodded towards the front page of the newspaper a man was reading on the other side of the aisle. One title read 'banned opposition parties still have followers'. Rachele had to show her husband she had got the message.

"So did I. I loved Mr Kron's theatre stories."

Rachele never liked the idea of a government banning political parties. Her family had been active in an 'unofficial organisation' in Trieste before World War I when it was still part of the Austrian empire. Back then, two of her brothers were active in an Italian national society the police had tried to ban. She was determined to have a confidential conversation with Alvise as soon as they could.

The two partners of the law firm knocked on her office's doorpost not long after she had sat down at her desk. They thought Rachele needed somebody else familiar with her clients besides the associate assigned to her. They knew Alvise was a close family friend, and they thought it would be easier for her to deal with him if she had to stop coming to the office earlier than planned. Rachele thanked them for their understanding.

She was still thinking how lucky she was. She loved her job. Not only she had a husband who supported her having a job even after Emma was born, she also worked for people who did not use her maternities as an excuse to terminate her employment. She picked up the revised contracts, stopped by Alvise's office on her way to the meeting room and asked him to join her for part of the meeting with Laszlo Kron, she'll ask the receptionist to call him; Alvise agreed.

Going through the contracts with Laszlo Kron was just a formality. A final review to make sure she had considered everything. She gave him the German translation of all the terms and conditions to take home, read, and let her know if she could send the signed Italian copy. She asked the receptionist to let Alvise know they were ready for him. When he joined them, she had to ask her clients if she could share the Italian version of the contracts with him, just so he was up to speed in case she had to stop coming to work earlier than planned.

The meeting was drawing to a close when the receptionist interrupted them saying there was an urgent call from Mario Dolfin. She transferred it to the meeting room. Rachele picked it up and Mario Dolfin came to the point.

"Please tell Laszlo Kron he has to come as soon as possible. The workers found a man in the garden shed. They have called an ambulance and the police."

Rachele related the message to Laszlo Kron, who asked her and Alvise to go with him.

"Mr Kron will be there as soon as possible. He asked Alvise Cantoni and I to come along as well. We'll be there as soon as we can."

"Would it help if I send one of the hotel speedboats?"

"It would save us time to organise a taxi. We could be ready at Rialto in fifteen to twenty minutes. I do not move as fast as I used to. "

"Don't worry, it would be at least half an hour before he is there."

Rachele related the conversation in German and Italian. On her way out to get her coat and her briefcase, she added,

"I wish we were there now. We may lose precious information if we arrive after they have removed him."

Then she had an idea

"Mr Kron, where is Dario Zago?"

"I sent him home. There were workers and cleaners and then I was going to move in. I thought he would like to be with his family. If you need him, ask Mario Dolfin."

She retraced her steps, picked up the phone and called the hotel Excelsior. Once they connected her to Mario Dolfin, she explained she needed to get in touch with Dario Zago, and it was urgent. He offered to do it for her.

"Thank you. Please tell him to go to Villa Kalman. If anybody asks, tell him to say he works as a researcher for Mr Kron's lawyers. He needs to talk to the workers who found the man, inspect the shed, and stay with the man until the ambulance or the police arrive."

"I'll tell him. He will be very excited to help."

"He has a keen sense of evidence and is an excellent observer. I need him to be my eyes and ears until we get there."

She then excused herself and went for her coat and briefcase. When the speedboat from the Hotel arrived, the three of them were there waiting.

Mindful of Rachele being at the last stages of pregnancy, Mario Dolfin also sent a car[2] to take them to the Villa. When they arrived, they noticed an ambulance from the local hospital; the police had not arrived yet. They found Dario Zago talking to the paramedics. He was telling them that as far as he knew the police had already been called. Dario clearly wanted to talk to Rachele, he excused himself just when Gino Moras arrived. He was in an agitated state; he noticed Rachele and Alvise standing by the entrance of the shed. Laszlo Kron had gone inside to get a chair for Rachele.

"One of those who work here came to tell me they found my brother badly beaten in the shed, how is he?"

The police arrived before anybody else could answer. Gino Moras looked at them and whispered to Alvise and Rachele.

"Now we are in trouble, my brother is a member of the Socialist party."

Alvise told him to calm down. The police went straight to Dario Zago, with a determination that prompted Rachele to intercept them. In her condition, it was next to impossible not to notice her.

"I am Avvocato Rachele Modiano Mendes, I work for the Venier-Zanin law firm, and I am the legal advisor to Mr Laszlo Kron, the owner of this Villa. This is Dario Zago a researcher for the firm, I asked him to come because we were notified of the discovery when Mr Kron and I were having a meeting at the firm's office near Rialto. He could be here faster than we could."

The policeman did not know what to do with a pregnant woman who claimed to be a lawyer. Rachele counted on that. It gave Dario time to collect himself and sound confident.

"I arrived after they had discovered there was a man in the shed. The cleaner who found him is in the kitchen, I am a second year law student. I know enough of the importance of evidence so I stopped anybody from going inside. When the ambulance arrived, I walked in with them to see if I could remember if they moved anything. We were careful not to tread over the trace of blood on the floor. There is a coat with a lot of blood by the door. The ambulance people are waiting for you to go in before they remove the young man. He has stopped bleeding and barely breathes, he seems asleep."

While Dario was talking to the police, Alvise had stopped Gino Moras from running inside the shed, he made sure he stayed there next to him. The senior police officer thanked him and went inside the shed followed by the medics.

Laszlo Kron arrived with a chair for Rachele, but Dario had a better idea. He told the policeman who was standing by the shed door they would be in the kitchen, pointing his head to Rachele and her big belly. He pointed at the window and told him to knock there when they were ready to talk to the cleaner who found the man.

As soon as Rachele entered the kitchen she became the centre of attention of the two ladies who were there. The one that was sitting down drinking water stood up to leave the chair to Rachele, it turned out she was the one who entered the shed and found the man. So Rachele had the chance to ask her what happened.

"I am not sure I should say these things to you. You are pregnant. You should only have nice thoughts."

Rachele took the woman's hands in hers.

"Thank you for your consideration, but I am a lawyer. I promise I only think of nice thoughts when I am home with my husband and my daughter. I understand you had the surprise of your life earlier."

The woman sat on the other chair.

"We were looking for a hose to clear the patio outside the music room, so I went in the shed to fetch it. I noticed what I thought were drops of tomato sauce by the door. When I saw the coat, I realised it was not tomato sauce."

Rachele noticed Dario was checking notes. He had obviously spoken to the lady before they arrived.

"That must have been distressing."

The cleaner nodded and continued

"It was, but it also made me think there was somebody who needed help. I followed the drops of blood and I found the man sitting on the lawn mower with his head on the gardener's workbench. I could see he was still breathing."

The other woman in the kitchen had refilled the glass of water and insisted that her colleague took a sip. Rachele interrupted the tale, partly to make sure she would take a sip or water.

"That must have been a relief."

The cleaner put down the glass of water.

"I crouched to look at his face. He looked asleep. I did not think of checking whether he was conscious. I just came out and called the foreman of the team of plumbers. He was the one who had the instructions of what to do in case of emergency. First, he called the Hotel to warn Mr Kron, then he called an ambulance. The person he spoke to said he would call the police."

Laszlo Kron whispered to Rachele

"Please act as her lawyer. I'll pay. We'll sort out the paperwork as soon as we can."

Rachele took Dario's notepad. Wrote 'wait by the door and tell me when the police come'. She then tore the piece of paper and put it in her briefcase. Dario stood up and moved by the door. Alvise looked at Rachele and nodded, so he moved to stand by the window. Rachele turned to the cleaner.

"Did you recognise the man?"

"I did not, but I was worried that the ambulance might take a long time, so when I saw Mrs Volpato, the retired midwife, in her garden. I asked her if she could come to look at him. Just in case he needed urgent help."

"Did she come?"

"She did. She noticed he was breathing but had stopped bleeding without moving him. She had seen somebody coming and going from the shed many times in the past few days."

Rachele looked at Alvise, who looked at Gino Moras. Alvise had been Gino's lawyer, so he asked Gino.

"How did you know it was your brother?"

Now Gino Moras felt deflated. He said in a low voice.

"The foreman of the team working here knows my brother. They used the shed as a safe place to meet. He had looked inside the shed from a window and he thought he recognised him. He wanted to go inside to check when Dario Zago stopped him, so he came to tell me."

Chapter Nine

December 1925

16 December 1925

Gino Moras had insisted on seeing Mr Kron, who had asked Mario Dolfin to join them because he wanted an independent witness. Laszlo Kron, Mario Dolfin, and Gino Moras were having coffee in a private room at the Hotel Excelsior. Gino Moras seemed to be more relaxed than the previous day, his new attitude surprised the other two.

"Yesterday, I went to the hospital and talked my way into seeing the young man your housekeeper found unconscious in Villa Kalman's garden shed. I was afraid he was my brother. They had washed him and I could tell he was not my brother. "

Mario Dolfin looked at Laszlo Kron, who nodded, showing he had understood.

"So, if he is not your brother, who is he?"

Laszlo Kron had every intention of finding out. He excused himself and went back to his room he had kept for one extra night and called Rachele, who shared her client's perplexity.

"Is the police still there?"

"No, they left late yesterday evening. I need to make sure the house is a safe place for my family, therefore I need to know who that man is and what he was doing in my garden shed."

Rachele paused for a few minutes.

"Dario Zago will come in about half an hour to sign the paperwork to work for us as a researcher. Do you mind if I send him to look at the shed?"

Laszlo Kron did not mind.

"It is a great idea. I am going to leave the hotel and move to the Villa. I'll be there in an hour. Tell him to look for the foreman if I am not there."

Rachele closed the conversation as fast as her manners allowed her to. She had to tell her boss that Dario Zago had already started billing for his time.

Dario Zago was happy he officially got the job as a researcher, paid by the hour. He could reconcile it with living at Villa Kalman when the Krons were not in residence. He also thought he could learn from Rachele and the other lawyers in the law firm. Overall, he could look at his next two years[1] with less financial concerns. He arrived at Villa Kalman and found Mr Kron in the kitchen talking to the housekeeper he had hired for two months. She was a friend of his mother's who worked in a hotel during the summer.

When he walked into the shed, the first thing he noticed was that the police had left the blood-stained coat. He looked inside the pockets and found the card of a guest-house in Cannareggio.[2] Maybe he would show it to the police if relevant. He had a torch with him and could see a wallet on the lower shelf of the workbench; the place was not well-lit, and it would have been easy for the police to miss it. He opened it and found some money (it was not an attempted robbery gone wrong), an identity card, and another strange document written in German. On his way out, he followed the blood traces between the workbench and the door of the shed. He went back to the kitchen and saw the housekeeper talking to another lady from the Lido who worked as a cook in a restaurant that was only open from Easter to October. They told him Mr Kron was in his study.

Laszlo Kron recognised the identity papers in German, unfortunately, his Italian was not good enough to discuss it with Dario Zago, so they called Rachele. Dario listened to the two of them having a conversation in German. He recognised a few words here and there, but could not follow. Mr Kron passed him the phone. After a few polite words, Rachele came straight to the point.

"I did not see the man. Do you think the Italian identity card is his?"

Dario looked at the card again.

"It could be. I did not see his face very well. I hope to go to the hospital tomorrow and try to visit him, so I can look at his face. Why?"

"Are you sure they took him to the Lido?"

"Where else? They came with an ambulance van, not an ambulance boat. It can only be the local hospital."

Dario could not see Rachele smile

"In that case, a close family friend, Paolo Mondani, works there. It should be his last month as an emergency nurse. He graduates as a doctor on Monday. I'll see if I can talk to him or his wife tonight and I'll ask him to help you. I'll call Mario Dolfin tomorrow, asking him to pass you a message."

Dario Zago thought the day the police accused him of shooting two teenagers was his lucky day. Rachele was a resourceful lawyer. He had a lot to learn from her.

"What about the German document?"

Rachele was waiting for that question.

"This is where things get interesting. It was a travel document issued by the Austrian Empire before World War I to allow young man who were old enough to be drafted into the Army to leave the territory of the empire temporarily. Did you find anything in the wallet that may tell us why he had it?"

Dario Zago looked at the content of the wallet again.

"The wallet contained cash, the two documents, a train ticket from Gorizia to Venice. I also found a card of the guest house where he is staying, 'Camere Crea', in Cannareggio."

Rachele was silent for a short time.

"Look at the Italian Identity Card. How old was he in 1915?"

"He would have been 17, but the German document is not his. There is a different name and a date of birth of 1895."

"Is there a photograph?"

"Wait a minute, I'll put a document under Mr Kron's desk lamp."

Dario opened the document and looked at the page where he expected to find a photograph.

"I think there was one originally. It is not there now."

Rachele had an idea but she needed to check with one of her brothers and with her honorary uncle first.

"Thank you. Can you come and see me tomorrow, after you have paid a visit to the hospital? Am I taking time away from your studies?"

Dario smiled.

"Avvocato Modiano, you are too young to be my mother. My next exams are in late February, so I have time. I'll check with Mario Dolfin by 10 am tomorrow. I'll come to see you in the afternoon. Mr Kron wants a word. Goodbye."

Rachele summarised her conversation with Dario Zago and told Mr Kron she had to make two calls to find out more about those travel permits, she will also have to contact the police to tell them about the wallet and the coat but she'll do it tomorrow morning. Meanwhile, it would help if he could copy the details in the two documents. Dario could help him with the Italian.

Once she had finished the conversation with her client and her research assistant, Rachele called her brother Daniele. Early in 1915, he and their brother Ricardo used one of those Austrian travel IDs. They travelled to Egypt and then to Italy to fight with the Italian side against the Austrian empire. The conversation was very important. Their father had bought two permits for them to travel to Alexandria, in Egypt. He gave them a letter and a small parcel for a business acquaintance, a Jewish man from Ancona who owned a café and a coffee roasting company, and another parcel they had to deliver to a villa in the Lido in Venice. At that stage, Rachele was very intrigued.

"Do you know what was in the parcels dad gave you? You made me wonder if our father was involved in some cloak and dagger business or if the mysterious man in Alexandria was a genuine business contact."

His brother paused for a moment.

"I don't know. If you are still curious, you could ask him in March when you come to my wedding. It turns out that they are Perla's uncle and aunt. They are coming to our wedding."

Rachele knew her brother had left that detail last on purpose.

"I'll do my best to have the baby on time so we can come to the wedding. Unless Perla has a problem having a baby and a toddler at the ceremony."

"I am sure she won't. Say hello to Gabriele and give Emma a hug from her uncle Daniele."

The couple in Alexandria being connected to her future sister-in-law was not the major surprise of the conversation. Daniele provided a link between the clandestine organisation helping Italian subjects of the Austrian Empire who wanted to fight for Italy and what had become Villa Kalman. Luckily, she had another source of information. She dialled the office number of her honorary uncle.

"Uncle Viktor, how are you? Do you have time? I think I need your help."

"Can you leave it till tomorrow? I could come to your office around 11."

"Perfect, I see you tomorrow."

The next and final call on the matter was to her friends Sofia and Paolo Mondani. Paolo picked up the phone.

"Congratulations, Doctor Mondani."

"It is still early. I have not graduated yet and I haven't sat for the exam to be licenced to practise medicine."

Rachele continued the light-hearted conversation for as short a time as she thought was appropriate and came to the point.

"Well, I am looking forward to celebrating Monday night. I can tell you without breaking confidence that there is a plot to have a big celebration. Fiamma, Anita, and your wife have been planning for over a month. They even dragged the countess into the committee."

Paolo laughed loud

"I am sure you did not call for that."

"No, I did not. I need a favour. Yesterday, a man was found semi-unconscious on the garden shed of my client's villa at the Lido…"

Paolo interrupted her

"Sorry to interrupt. Do you mean the one found in Villa Kalman's garden?"

"That one, we have found his wallet and my researcher, Dario Zago, will deliver it to the police tomorrow morning. He also needs to have a word with the man, or if he is still unconscious to make sure that the wallet is his. Can you smuggle him in?"

Paolo thought for a minute.

"I have the early shift. Tell him to show up after 10 am, ask for me and be prepared to wait."

"Thank you. I will pass on the message. See you on Monday."

"You will see us on Saturday. Aunt Fiamma has invited us to lunch."

"Even better, give my best to Sofia and hugs to Arrigo from his aunt Rachele and uncle Gabriele."

Chapter Ten

December 1925

17 December 1925

It was Gabriele's turn to supervise Emma's breakfast. However, Rachele could not linger in bed. She had to start on the biscuits for Shabbat. The whole Mendes clan was expecting her Kipferl and her chocolate biscuits. Preparation was well underway when Anita came back from the fish market.

"I met the Rabbi's wife at the market. We are planning the same lunch, except her recipe for lemon sole is more interesting."

Emma was making sure that her mouth and her spoon met at the right moment and that all the food was going inside her mouth. Rachele noticed that the floor under the table was clean. A rare event. She pointed the floor to Anita, who smiled and nodded. Anita also met Fiamma at the market.

"Fiamma and I treated us to a coffee at a café near the fish market, the one by the ferry. She told me that your honorary aunt told her you were seeing her husband this morning. Fiamma wants you to remind him dinner is at them this week."

Rachele was kneading the dough for the biscuits.

"I am sure Aunt Deborah will remind him, but I'll find a tactful way to tell him as well."

~

When Rachele arrived at work, she needed something warm. She was longing for a coffee, but she knew her stomach would not appreciate it. Therefore, she decided to make herself a hot chocolate. Alvise was in the kitchen. They both moaned about the weather for a few minutes, and then Rachele asked him if he had time at 11 to sit in the meeting with her uncle. If he had time, she would like to spend ten minutes with him beforehand to share some recent developments with him. She then added with a mischievous grin that the man in the shed was not Gino Moras' brother. They will know the man in the shed's identity before 11 am if Dario rings her before Count Viktor Pesaro de Bonfili arrives, or as soon as he leaves, if Dario calls later. A very intrigued Alvise Cantoni ensured he would find the time.

~

Dario Zago called around 10.30, leaving plenty of time to update Alvise.

"I have been to the hospital. You did not tell me that Paolo Mondani will graduate on Monday. I thought they were congratulating him because his wife had a baby! Anyway, our man had not regained consciousness yet, but I looked at his face very well."

Rachele was not exactly impatient, but she was eager to have an identification and a name.

"And?"

"He is Thomas Donda, born in Gorizia in 1897, the document in German was made out to a Franz Donda born in Gorizia in 1894, he would have been twenty when World War I broke out, but, as you know, Italy joined the war in 1915."

Rachele asked Dario to wait a minute. She needed to check she had the right names. It was important. Once she checked she did, she asked him to come to the office as soon as possible. If she was busy, wait for her. Then she called Laszlo Kron and told him she hoped they needed to come to the villa in the afternoon.

Once she put down the phone, she sat back in her chair, the two index fingers joined and touching her lips, her eyes closed. Those who worked closely with her knew it was her 'thinking pose'. The first question she had to answer was the connection between Franz Donda and the Villa. She had an idea and hoped her honorary uncle might help.

At a quarter to eleven, Alvise appeared so she could update him on the latest events. They had almost finished when the receptionist came to tell her that Count Pesaro de Bonfili had arrived. She picked up a fresh notepad and got up and invited Alvise to join her and her honorary uncle in the meeting room with a partial view of Rialto Bridge. Rachele kept the social side of the conversation as short as her manners allowed.

"Aunt Deborah told me that Laszlo Kron bought what is now Villa Kalman from the estate of one of your cousins. Something has happened that may go back to the time when he was alive and owned the Villa, so I thought you are my best source of information, or at least I hope you are."

Count Viktor Pesaro De Bonfili finished his coffee.

"Happy to help as much as I can."

Rachele told him about the man found in the shed and the documents they had found in his wallet. Almost at the end of her summary, her honorary uncle's facial expression changed.

"Did you say he had an Austrian travel document in his wallet? I am not sure whether it is relevant but I can link that to my cousin, Isacco Bloch. He was the son of my aunt Sarah, my father's older sister. He was your father's friend and, if I remember correctly, he introduced us long before you were born."

Isacco's wife was originally from Trieste. Around 1910, her brother became the president of the Adriatic Club, whose secret purpose was to foster Italian nationalism in Trieste, and the whole Italian-speaking part of the Austrian empire. Until 1914 they were mostly a cultural organisation, but after Franz Ferdinand[1] was killed at Sarajevo, they started helping Italian young men who wanted to fight on the Italian side if Italy entered the war. The Count did not know how they got hold of blank travel permits and an official stamp, but they did. Rachele's two brothers, Daniele and Ricardo used them to travel to Italy.[2] Young men with no connection in Italy would often stay at Isacco Bloch's home. His wife had died, his daughters were married and living somewhere else, and his son had moved to Padua to live closer to the factory. He was alone in the Villa and he had told his staff that he had joined a European Jewish organisation offering shelter to young men who were travelling. His housekeeper, who was the aunt of the Pesaro De Bonfili housekeeper, told them she thought he did that because he was lonely.

Alvise saw Rachele taking notes, with no changes in facial expression. When the count had finished telling the story, he noticed that her facial expression changed. It was clear she had realised the personal angle in the story once she had stopped taking notes and allowed herself to relax. Rachele put down her pen and took a sip of water.

"Uncle Viktor, was my father involved in the Adriatic club?"

"Rachele, that is not my story to tell."

Count Viktor realised that his answer might have given away more than he had wanted. He made a mental note to call his friend in Trieste to warn him. He just hoped that his honorary niece was too busy in the next couple of hours to call her father.

Alvise and the count could see in Rachele's facial expression that she had taken a mental note, filed it somewhere in her mind and was focusing again on the man in the shed.

"Do you know if something else was going on in the Villa besides hosting people who had arrived in Venice from the empire?"

"I was not part of the organisation, so I only know what my cousin shared with me. However, it is entirely possible that he kept things in the villa, somewhere where his staff would not normally go. Something that would help those young men or would help the cause of bringing the 'unredeemed lands'[3] into the Italian fold."

Rachele paused, as she always did before she asked an important question.

"Do you have any idea where that somewhere could be?"

A long pause followed the question. Rachele's honorary uncle was going through his memories of the Villa. He thought of the old changing room when there was a tennis court in the garden. Isacco Bloch had the tennis court removed when his wife became unwell and was confined in a wheelchair. A paved patio with a pergola replaced the tennis court, so they could easily wheel his wife outside whenever she wished.

"I am not sure if the current owner has kept the fence between the tradesmen's area and the garden. If it is still there, look at the part of the shed beyond the fence. There is a door. I would start looking from there."

Alvise remembered the fence

"There is a fence that starts from the corner of the villa and ends on the long wall of the garden shed, almost two-thirds of the way in."

Count Viktor smiled.

"That's the fence I mean."

Rachele's face lit up.

"Thank you, Uncle Viktor. You have been helpful beyond my wildest expectations."

18 December 1925

Rachele was drinking her hot chocolate in her office, she was happy she had explained to Dario Zago and Laszlo Kron what they had to look for. Being seven months pregnant meant she had to manage her energy and her movement and there was no way she would have coped with a trip to the Lido on a Friday in December and the stress of being home to be ready for Shabbat before sunset.[4] She was also curious to see what they would find and had given strict instructions to call her office before 2pm or if they needed more time to let her know Saturday evening after nightfall. Laszlo Kron was a secular Jew, but he understood the rules Rachel was following, so she gave him her home phone number just in case they would have found nothing by 2pm.

Dario Zago and Laszlo Kron had been looking at the back of the shed for a while before they realised that two overgrown rose bushes had hidden a paved path. They followed the short path and found a door that Mr Kron did not know existed. The first thing they thought was that Thomas Donda, the man who was unconscious at the hospital, did not know it existed either, otherwise, he would have hidden there rather than where they found him.

Nobody had opened that door for at least three years. It was not locked, but it was difficult to open it. When Dario pried it open, he found a switch. He tried it. The light was still working. Walking inside, the first thing he noticed was a window that had been blocked with plaster and a skylight that nobody had noticed because it was hidden by the branches of two trees, one in the Villa's garden and another one in the neighbouring property. There were shower stalls and a toilet to the left of the door and, to the right, there was a sort of temporary accommodation with two campbeds and a desk. Dario reckoned that Isacco Bloch had turned the changing area into temporary accommodations for young Italians who were Austrian citizens but had decided to fight for Italy rather than against Italy. Dario reckoned it would be difficult to lift usable fingerprints after at least seven years, if not longer, so he and Laszlo Kron started searching the room. The area where the campbeds were, revealed nothing beyond dusty blankets and old pillows. The desk drawer had blank sheets of paper, pens, and nothing else. Dario started looking at the shower and changing rooms. The toilet had a grating rather than a window. The goal was to give air to the toilet, with no visibility from the outside. It was also high up, very close to the ceiling. Dario climbed on the toilet seat to search the water tank and noticed a bag on the inside windowsill where the grating was. He took down the bag; the dust made him cough. He climbed down from the toilet seat, opened it and found what looked like a diary, a few old notes, photos, and a smaller notepad that looked like an address book. One photo showed a young man with a teenager. The young man looked like Thomas Donda. Dario and Mr Kron agreed it must have been a photo of Thomas with his older brother Franz.

They left the changing rooms and closed the door. Laszlo Kron would think about what to do with the space later; meanwhile, he would have it cleaned, re-open the blocked window, and put a lock on the door. The diary was written in

German, he would read it during the weekend and maybe go with Dario to meet Rachele on Monday morning. He asked Dario to come back Monday morning to go with him to see Rachele and give her the diary, the notepad, and the photos. Once he was alone, he went back to his study and called Rachele at work to update her.

Chapter Eleven

December 1925

21 December 1925

Rachele was at the stage of pregnancy where she needed to visit the toilet very often. Her second meeting with Dario Zago was getting uncomfortable. Alvise could see her fidgeting. Memories of his wife's pregnancy came back, and he was wondering whether Rachele could focus while she needed to go to the toilet. He was looking at Rachele with some concern. She could see his concern but did not want to smile, nod, or make other reassuring gestures Dario could misinterpret.

"Just to summarise, Thomas Donda woke up this morning. He is now conscious, but very weak. Does he remember what happened?"

Now Dario had noticed Rachele's fidgeting as well. He was the eldest of five. He remembered his mother's last two pregnancies and could guess why Rachele was fidgeting.

"I told him that now he had a lawyer, the owner of the house had agreed to pay for it. I also told him I would go back tomorrow with a copy of the paperwork. Thomas told me he felt very tired. The doctor told me to go back tomorrow if I wanted to ask him anything. Would you like a break? My mother needed it when she started looking like you look now."

Rachele wanted to ask him how he thought she looked, but then she saw Alvise's face and excused herself. Five minutes later, she was back, looking more relaxed.

"Did you talk to a doctor about how he is?"

"No, but your friend Paolo Mondani did. He told me he was stable. The wound is healing well and the internal bleeding seems to have stopped. He has lost a lot of blood. There is no further internal damage they can see, but there are a lot of bruises and a few cracked ribs. The police will investigate what they called 'the event' without the need of somebody pressing charges."

Rachele thanked Dario and told him the receptionist had a copy of the paperwork proving that Thomas Donda had legal representation and who was paying for it. He should pick it up on his way out and remember to take it with him the following day. Thomas Donda needed a copy handy just in case the police were not just interested in him as a victim.

When the meeting was over, the receptionist told her that Gabriele had rung to say that he would be half an hour late and Franco Venier wanted to see her.

Rachele had been feeling like an inflated balloon for a few weeks. According to the midwife, she was not too large for the seventh month of pregnancy, but she felt it. She declined to sit on the couch in Franco Venier's office. She preferred the chair. Rachele hoped her boss was so supportive because she had proved to be an excellent lawyer and not because she was also good at bringing clients to the firm thanks to her connections and her family's connections.

"I asked you to come to see me because I wanted to give you the good news in person. Mario Dolfin called me. We are the new legal advisors of Hotel Excelsior. He asked you to be the lead. Do you mind if I put myself as a second name?"

Rachele did not think she had had the opportunity to show her legal skills to Mario Dolfin. Maybe he was impressed by the way she handled the two teen-age boys, Dario Zago, and Laszlo Kron.

"Why should I mind? After all, if things go well, I'll take a three-month leave of absence starting from the end of January."

Franco Venier hoped to sound caring and supportive rather than cynical.

"And I promised Gabriele I'll make sure you do not end up walking all around Venice in the next five weeks. Just to be open, I want to be the second name because I want the perks."

Rachele adjusted her posture.

"Mario Dolfin told me about the perks."

"I did not expect to have free use of all the daytime facilities of the Hotel Excelsior, and have 'staff rates' at the restaurants and bars of the hotel."

"I know what you mean. We are looking forward to making use of their beach next summer."

Alvise and Gabriele knocked on the doorpost. It was time to go home. The three men offered to help Rachele stand, she was not impressed.

"I may be as big as a whale, but I can still stand with no help. That is why I sit on chairs rather than armchairs."

Gabriele stuck with his plan to replace the walk home with a short walk, vaporetto, and another walk. He thought it would be slower but easier on Rachele. Rachele's size made sure many passengers offered their seats. They talked about Emma, who had started creating sentences and she was only about two months away from her second birthday.

22 December 1925

Rachele was spending the morning reading in her office. She had an armchair moved from one of her meeting rooms to her office to become her footstool. She planned to read most of the morning and therefore keep her feet up most of the morning. She had started from the address book that Dario Zago had retrieved, hoping to find some names she expected, like Isacco Bloch. However, she did not expect to see her brothers' names, each one of them next to another name. She picked up the phone and rang her brother Daniele and came straight to the point after the shortest social interaction her manners allowed.

"I am looking at an address book which may date back to the early days of World War I. Your name and Ricardo's name are in it. Each one of you has another name next to it. You have a Dino Monari, Ricardo has a Renato Marini. Who are they?"

Daniele did not expect that conversation. He had not thought of the choice he and his brother had made to fight for Italy, instead of against Italy, as their birthplace would have dictated.

"It is a long story."

"My dear brother, I have my feet up, I have all the time you need."

Daniele never figured out why he never mentioned the story before. He was sure his parents knew, but he'd better check later and maybe tell the story twice.

"When we arrived in Italy in 1914, the Italian office of the organisation that helped us cross the border was near the harbour in Venice. They checked we were not speaking Italian

97

with a German accent, they gave us an Italian identity and sent us to a Villa at the Lido, where we were given further instructions and an Italian ID under our assumed Italian name."

Rachele interrupted her brother.

"So, in the Italian Army, you were Dino Monari?"

"Yes, and our brother was Renato Marini, they tried to keep the same initials. They thought it would be easier for us to remember our new name."

Rachele was beginning to figure out what was going on in the Villa in late 1914 and early 1915.

"So when I see two names next to each other, one is the real name and the other one was the name given for the purpose of joining the Italian military."

Daniele Modiano's voice became more lively

"They did that to avoid us being sentenced for treason."

"Did it work?"

Daniele Modiano's voice became sad.

"Not with everybody. For instance, a Slav schoolmate recognised Nazario Sauro[1], after they took him as a prisoner of war with other Italian soldiers."

Rachele became curious, there were a few pieces of the whole organisation still missing.

"How did you and Ricardo know to come to Venice?"

Daniele was hesitant, he wondered whether there was a reason their father never discussed it with his sisters.

"Dad and Michele were part of the Circolo Adriatico[2], in the club's basement there was a political organisation that was working towards Trieste becoming part of Italy. Our father used his friendship with your honorary uncle and his business connection with his cousin. On this end, they had contacts with a forger who could help when the emergency travel documents could not be obtained in any other way."

Now Rachele was not sure whether she was talking to her brother or a witness.

"Did you know Franz Donda?"

"Do you mean the young man from Gorizia who was distributing paperwork and organising appointments with the army? I can't say I knew him, but I think I just described what he was doing in Venice."

Rachele had called her brother because she saw his name in the address book. She did not expect him to provide so much information.

"I think so. His younger brother is in hospital because he was beaten up. We have retrieved an address book, a diary, and other items from what used to be a changing room in a villa at the Lido that is now called Villa Kalman. The new owner did not know the door to the changing room existed."

Daniele had in store an even bigger surprise for Rachele.

"Ricardo would know more about him. He arrived in Venice a few weeks before I did, it's a long story. Call him, maybe try calling him tonight at home."

Rachele thanked her brother. She needed time to write one of her diagrams to sort out the information she had received from her brother, and she hadn't even started on the diary.

It took her three phone calls to her father, her brother and her honorary uncle Viktor to put together the story of the organisation she did not know existed until that morning. Nobody could tell her what happened to Franz Donda. She may have to wait to hear what Dario Zago had found out from his younger brother.

Countess Deborah interrupted Rachele's morning. She had agreed to go with her to her dressmaker for the final fitting of her elegant maternity clothes. Luckily, it was just a ten minutes' walk across the Rialto bridge. On the way, she asked her aunt if she had an idea what her husband's cousin was up to during World War I.

"Isacco was the eldest child of Viktor's father's eldest sister. He was at least twenty years older than Viktor, he had several hobbies. I do not know how he spent his time, talk to my husband."

Rachele concluded the men had decided not to share their cloak-and-dagger activities with the women of the family. She decided to take a break from Villa Kalman's secrets and enjoy the fitting.

Alvise was looking at Rachele's diagrams, a technique she had learnt from one of her professors at university.

"We now understand from your brothers what was going on at Villa Kalman between October 1914 and September 1916. We also understand that Franz Donda simply disappeared. Thomas thought he was dead and buried under a different name."

Rachele continued

"Except all changed when at the beginning of this year, a man who had fought for Italy in WWI came to the bank where Thomas was working to seek a loan to buy his home. When the man asked him if he was related to Franz Donda, Thomas asked if he had any idea under which name his brother was buried. Thomas got the surprise of his life when his clients told him that Franz had never served on the front. He kept his role in the background until he disappeared in September 1916."

Alvise looked at the diagram

"Now we have somebody shooting at two teenagers from inside the Villa and somebody beating up Thomas Donda almost to his death. What are we missing?"

Rachele pointed to a circle with no notes

"We are missing what Thomas was doing between the time he arrived and the time Mr Kron's housekeeper found him in the shed semi-unconscious. We also have not been where he is staying in Venice."

Rachele retrieved a business card from a folder

"Here it is, *Camere Crea* in Cannareggio. I need to send Dario to visit him again tomorrow morning."

Rachele called Mario Dolfin, one of her ways to send a message to Dario Zago. She told him what he had to find out. After his visit, he should come straight to the office to discuss his conversations before he forgot any details.

On her way home, Rachele was in an excellent mood. It was a clear night, and they enjoyed the vaporetto ride on the Grand Canal. Gabriele sensed his wife needed to relax. He did not break the silence between them. He just enjoyed sitting next to her, her head on his shoulder, his arms around her shoulder. When it was time to get off, somebody offered to help Rachele. As they were walking home, Rachele broke her silence.

"Am I so big that everybody treats me as if I were a delicate Chinese vase?"

Gabriele knew he had to think quickly.

"People around you care for your well-being. You are carrying another life inside you."

Rachele smiled, tightened her grip on her husband's arm

"Wrong answer. I did not ask you why people are so nice to me. I asked you if I am that big."

Now it was Gabriele's turn to smile

"I decline to answer that question because my life could be at risk. I want to see Emma and the new one grow up."

"You know, you almost spoke like a lawyer."

"Maybe something rubbed off since I married you."

Rachele tried to kiss him on the cheek. Unfortunately, her movements were not as swift as they used to be. They had to stop walking to allow her to kiss her husband's cheek.

"You see, I am big."

When they arrived home, they were greeted by a toddler running towards them. Gabriele intercepted Emma before she could crash against her mother's belly. He picked her up, hugged her, talked to her while Anita was helping Rachele with her coat and then passed Emma on to her mother, who gave her another hug and a kiss. Then Anita took her from her mother and put her down. Rachele noticed for the first time how co-ordinated the other two were, almost as if they had been doing it for a while and she only noticed that evening.

23 December 1925

It was a chilly but cloudless morning, one of those that are unusual in December but fairly common in January. The sun was shining but was not doing much to make Gabriele and Rachele feel warmer on their walk to the vaporetto stop. The streets were more crowded than usual. They had to greet people they knew and couldn't really have a conversation. It was only when they were sitting inside in the vaporetto that Rachele felt she could ask the question.

"We have a long weekend. This year Christmas comes on a Friday. Normally, it means nothing to us. However, this year we have the usual family commitments on Shabbat. So Friday dinner and Shabbat lunch are with family. We have Paolo, Sofia, and Arrigo for dinner on 26th. Do you think it can be just us on the 27th?"

Gabriele was looking at the front page of somebody else's paper. He turned to look at his wife.

"I like the idea of one day just us. If it is a day like today, we may spend some time sitting on a bench in the Campo and watch Emma run around."

"Or try to run around. "

They both smiled, thinking of the scene.

"Alvise and I usually work to allow our Christian colleagues some time off. Talk to Viola and arrange a time for Franco and Emma to play next week. If you do not want to be seen in public with a woman that is not your wife, ask Anita to be your chaperone."

"I might have to work, too. We could ask Anita if she minds looking after two children one afternoon and give Viola a break."

Rachele was silent for a few minutes.

"We are very lucky to have Anita, which reminds me tonight we have to buy a present for her. I have seen something I think she might like in a shop in Calle Larga. We might take a detour on our way home tonight."

"If we can't, show me the shop. I have to take leave otherwise I lose it. I might take tomorrow off and go there tomorrow morning."

By then, they had arrived outside Rachele's office. Gabriele kissed his wife on the cheek, hugged her and left to walk to his office. She stood there watching him until he turned the corner, then started climbing the stairs to her first floor office, thinking that she was a very lucky woman and life had been very good to her.

Rachele, Alvise, and Dario Zago were in Rachele's office. Dario loved being considered a member of staff, no meeting room for him. He had a lot to tell them. Thomas' conditions were improving, but they reckoned he needed at least another week before they could discharge him.

"He remembered very little of the last couple of days before he was beaten up, but he had a diary in his room. He told me his room number and where he has left the envelope with the money. Laszlo Kron has decided Thomas will convalesce at Villa Kalman. So, tomorrow I am going with a policeman to his hotel room to pay, pack his things, check him out, and take his things to Villa Kalman."

Rachele was taking notes. Alvise stopped writing.

"Who had the idea of the policeman?"

"Laszlo Kron had discussed things with me and Mario Dolfin this morning before I went to the hospital. Mario Dolfin thought that going there with a policeman would give me credibility. After all, I had to gain access to his room, pay, leave with all his things, and take them to Villa Kalman."

Rachele stopped taking notes

"You said he had a diary. Can you take the diary to me tomorrow morning? The office is open until lunchtime."

Alvise had a better idea

"What if I meet you outside his hotel or guesthouse? I'll help you pack and come away with his diary while you distract the policeman, who may consider it evidence in whatever they are investigating if they are investigating."

Chapter Twelve

January 1926

2 January 1926

A week earlier Gabriele and Rachele did not expect to see the Kron family crossing the bridge between the Campo del Ghetto Novo and Calle del Ghetto Vecchio.[1] Gabriele's father, Samuele Mendes, instinctive reaction was to invite them for lunch. Laszlo Kron's wife declined saying that there were five of them, Gabriele's mother would not have liked such an unplanned invasion. Samuele insisted they had to come to lunch the following Saturday. So the Krons had joined the Mendeses and the Pesaro De Bonfilis on their walk to Gabriele's parents' home following the synagogue service. When Rachele introduced Count Viktor Pesaro De' Bonfili, she mentioned that her uncle's cousin was the previous owner of Villa Kalman. Laszlo Kron had read Franz Donda's diary and was curious about Isacco Bloch, luckily the two men were both fluent in French.

"I read about what happened in your cousin's home during World War I. We found a diary in a changing room I did not know existed."

Initially, Count Viktor could not understand how Laszlo Kron could not know about the changing room. Then the proverbial penny dropped.

"Isacco might have built it without extending the shed, so he may not have changed the official drawing deposited with the Land Registry. Rachele and I talked about the diary two or three weeks ago. It did not last until the end of World War I. My cousin stopped hosting the operation when the young man who was running it suddenly disappeared in the autumn of 1916."

Laszlo Kron thought Rachele ought to know about that.

"Did you discuss it with Rachele?"

"It did not come up in our conversation, please don't mention it to her today. She does not like to talk about work on the Sabbath."

Laszlo Kron told the count he understood, but he planned to tell Rachele after sunset.[2] It was too important.

4 January 1926

It was Gabriele's turn to supervise Emma's breakfast. Rachele appeared in the kitchen about twenty minutes after Emma started breakfast wearing one of the two maternity dresses that her aunt's dressmaker had prepared. Anita was ready with a hot chocolate.

"You look very elegant. Are you due in court?"

Rachele kissed Emma, groaned as she stood up after bending, and grabbed the cup with the hot chocolate.

"No, I am just celebrating the beginning of the countdown to my three months' leave. Although I told Franco Venier that I would be available to look at some contracts during that time, but nothing urgent."

Gabriele kept looking at Emma but was replying to his wife.

"Didn't they tell you that 'leave' means 'leave from work'?"

Rachele rolled her eyes, and looked at Anita, silently seeking support, but found none.

"I understand that. Except, I remember being really bored when I stayed home when Emma was born. I thought I could take a bit of time each day to look at something."

She got up and went to Emma and took her face in her hands

"Although this time I have Emma to keep me entertained and make sure I am not bored. Emma, will you help mummy?"

Emma did not enjoy somebody squeezing her cheeks, so she said no and pulled one of her mother's hands away. Rachele's face turned serious, which made Emma look serious again. Gabriele, fearing a drama at the beginning of the day, felt he had to intervene.

"I am sure she just said no because she thought you would squeeze her cheeks like my mother does. Emma hates it."

Then turned to Emma with a big grin on his face

"Isn't it Emma? You do not like it when Grandma Fiamma squeezes your cheeks."

Emma saw her father smile and smiled. Crisis averted, Gabriele turned to Anita.

"Let's start the countdown. Two weeks and two days to go until 20 January, Rachele's last day at the office before she gives birth."

Anita was checking the pantry. She emerged holding a pen and paper.

"I marked it in the calendar. Is there anything you wish I'd buy at the market? Myriam comes to play with Emma this morning. I go shopping when she is here."

Gabriele could not think of anything; Rachele asked her to buy coffee-flavoured chocolate.

"I do not understand why this time coffee gives me nausea, anyway I miss it. Let's see if I can at least have coffee-flavoured chocolate."

Anita looked at Gabriele who rolled his eyes and nodded.

Rachele was looking at a contract when the office telephone operator called her to tell her Antonio Penzo was on the line asking for her. Three years earlier, he was weary of a married upper-class woman who wanted to practise law; since then, he had become an admirer of Rachele's knowledge of the law, her investigative abilities, and her judgement of people.

"They assigned me the case of Thomas Donda. After listening to the police, I have to decide whether to investigate who beat him up so badly to leave him unconscious or do nothing since he seems to recover. I understand you are his legal counsel. Can I come and talk to you this afternoon?"

Rachele checked her diary to see when she was supposed to meet with Dario Zago and Alvise Cantoni.

"I am available around 4. Do you mind if our researcher and Alvise Cantoni join us? Alvise will take over my cases when I start my three months' leave in a couple of weeks."

Antonio Penzo agreed but added he may like a second conversation just with her, maybe the following morning on the phone. Rachele did not mind.

Rachele decided it was time to call her father. She shook her head thinking that this case, if there was a case, would involve her family. Her father was available.

After enquiring about her parents' health, she asked her father whether her brother Daniele had talked to him about their conversation. When Baron Davide Modiano told her he had, she came straight to the point.

"I need to discuss what was going on in the basement of the Circolo Adriatico. When did things end?"

"We had a system to communicate with Venice via Switzerland using telegrams. I received a telegram from our Swiss contact telling us to stop sending people. Isacco Bloch's message was clear. The young man who was creating Italian identities had vanished. He was concerned somebody might have kidnapped him or even killed him."

"Do you remember when was that?"

"I am not sure of an exact date, I remember it was before Rosh HaShanah.[3]"

Rachele opened Franz Donda's diary. The last entry was on 24 September 1916.

"What happened to the young men who had started the journey but not yet arrived in Venice?"

Baron Modiano went silent for a while

"I think we stopped the last two, but we never found out what happened to the other six."

Rachele's father's tone of voice left no doubt about what he thought happened to them.

Rachele read the last entry in the diary. Franz was describing the person he was about to meet. He also wrote that he had cleaned his gun the previous evening, he thought he might have to take it with him.

Rachele was beginning to have an idea, but she did not know how to prove it. She wanted a second opinion, so she made another phone call. She apologised for her lack of manners, but she came straight to the point.

"Good morning Mr Kron, can you do me a favour?"

"What do you need?"

"Do you have time to come tomorrow to my office, I am sorry but I'd rather not make the journey to the Lido. I need you to read the last two pages of Franz's diary and then I need to ask your opinion."

Rachele summarised what her father had told her to Dario Zago and Alvise Cantoni. Then she shared her theory with them. She thought they could find the key to what happened the previous December once they figured out what happened during World War I. Many Italian subjects of the Austrian empire believed that the Italian-speaking territories of the empire, the so-called 'unredeemed lands', ought to be part of Italy. A clandestine operation was helping young men from those areas come to Italy, acquire an Italian identity, join the Army and fight for Italy against Austria. They would leave Austria using real or counterfeit special travel permits, the basement of the Circolo Adriatico in Trieste was one of the starting points of their journey. The house they knew as Villa Kalman was one of the arrival points. Isacco Bloch was only providing the home and maybe some logistic help. The real core of the operation was Franz Donda. When he disappeared, the Venetian end of the entire operation was closed.

"We'll never know why Isacco Bloch closed the operations in Venice. Based on what my father told me, he sent a few distressed and urgent messages to Trieste. I read Franz's diary and I think he was eliminated. If we find the person who killed him, we also find the person who beat his brother, Thomas, unconscious."

Alvise was the first to react.

"Your theory is plausible. Do you have any further information from the diary?"

Rachele picked up Franz Donda's diary and started translating the last page into Italian

"I am going to meet somebody who claims he can open a faster route to allow people to cross the border. I have to talk to him, but I have an uneasy feeling. If it is a trap and I do not come back, whoever takes over from me should know that Marasich is an assumed name and he is the reason I did not come back."

She closed the diary and looked at the two men with a metaphorical quotation mark on her face. Alvise was the first to react.

"Is there any description of Mr Marasich or of the place where they met?"

Rachele almost smiled. It was clear she had a theory, and she was not ready to share it just yet.

"No, but I think that whoever Mr Marasich is, he killed Franz in 1916 and almost beat Thomas to death in December 1925. We find him, we solve two crimes in one go."

Dario had been writing something on his notepad while he was listening.

"What makes you think Mr Marasich, or whatever his real name is, still lives in Venice? To be responsible for the murder and the beating up, as you just said, he must live in Venice."

Rachele showed him her circle-based mind map.

"Thomas was in Venice to find out what happened to his brother. Unless my pregnancy has wrecked my brain, I do not think he has shared with us why he was beaten up. Therefore, I am inclined to assume that he got too close to finding the person who had information about what happened to his brother."

Alvise looked at Dario.

"When he was in hospital, the doctors told me to avoid distressing him. When he was out of hospital, my mother and Mrs Kron were very protective and always ready to tell me to stop if he looked distressed."

Rachele had an idea

"Do you want me to talk to your mother and Mrs Kron? Whatever happens, you may be more gentle than a policeman or a junior magistrate."

"Anything may help, but I would like to try again. If I leave now, I'll be there early enough to talk to him before dinner. Today it is my mother's turn to look after him. I may talk her into leaving me alone with him."

Rachele told Dario it was a good idea. He stood up and put his coat on. Before he left the room, they wished him good luck. Once they were alone in the room, Rachele had something else she wanted to discuss with Alvise.

"Is Gino Moras still our client?"

"Not anymore. Why?"

"This is a gut feeling that may lead us nowhere fast. Can we establish if he has a brother and if his brother was a member of the banned Socialist Party?"

Alvise looked at his friend. He could almost see her mind working overtime.

"I need to talk to Laszlo Kron before I explain my theory. Let's say that he has mentioned a brother each time he appeared at Villa Kalman. However, we have never seen a brother."

Alvise was beginning to see where Rachele's mind was heading towards.

"I can try to find out if a Moras was a member of the banned Socialist party in Venice, I know people. I would also like to find the foreman, who, according to Gino Moras, informed him his brother was in the shed. It might have been his excuse to show up when all he wanted to check was whether his victim was alive."

Rachele dropped her notepad and her pen, opened her arms in a gesture of mock triumph.

"I knew there must have been a reason why an hour after Gabriele introduced us, I felt I had known you forever. We have the same twisted mind."

Alvise smiled, shrugged his shoulders, and said,

"Maybe that's why we became lawyers."

Rachele knew she had to ask Antonio Penzo to return the following day at the same time. She did not cancel the meeting because she hoped to find out what he knew, and it might have been too late to cancel. She invited her boss, Franco Venier, to be in the meeting, because he was a good friend of the magistrate and might help to convince him it was worth his while to wait.

There was no way Rachele could hide her pregnancy, so she sort of expected Antonio Penzo's reaction. He stood up and the moment he saw her belly he started asking how she was and shouldn't she be at home, given her state. He received her standard reply.

"I am pregnant. I am not sick. My leave starts in about two weeks. Alvise will take care of my clients when I am at home. May we include him in our meeting? "

It was a way to buy some time and assess whether the magistrate would mind returning the following day. Antonio Penzo waited for Alvise Cantoni to arrive before he started explaining why he had asked for the meeting.

"Thomas Donda's wounds were too serious to wait for his decision whether to press charges. By law, we had to investigate. When I noticed your name as his legal representative, I thought it would save time if I came and talked to you before I started."

Rachele asked him to be patient because she had to start from the beginning. She explained how she found out what Thomas' brother, Franz, was up to between 1914 and 1916, and how they discovered his diary. She also told him the diary was in German and she had read it.

"Thomas came to Venice to find out what happened to his brother. We believe Franz was killed. I think that if you find his killer, you also find the person who beat Thomas Donda unconscious."

Antonio Penzo had been taking notes. He lifted his head from his notepad.

"Do you think you know where to look?"

Rachele expected that question. She looked at Alvise and at her boss. They both nodded as a sign of support.

"Could you come back tomorrow? There are a couple of things that I need to check before I can formulate a theory. At the moment, all I have is a gut feeling. I'd rather wait until we have spoken to a few people."

She could see the question mark on the magistrate's face.

"Our researcher, Alvise, and I will speak to three different people by tomorrow lunchtime. Come tomorrow at the same time and I'll have a theory, and I hope I'll have some evidence as well. But there is something you can check better than any of us could. I promise I'll explain everything tomorrow."

Chapter Thirteen

January 1926

5 January 1926

When Anita walked into the kitchen, she found Rachele in the middle of putting the basis for a pistachio pie in the mould. Rachele did not even lift her head.

"I'll sort this mess out in about ten minutes, then I'll get Emma."

Anita was looking for the coffee. She turned around and found the jar on the table.

"I am not worried about that. I am concerned because you are up early and baking. You shouldn't be anxious."

Rachele noticed Anita picking up the jar of coffee.

"Sorry, I meant to put it back. I am experimenting with a layer of coffee-flavoured cream underneath the pistachio cream. Today I should find out if my gut feeling was correct, or if I was about to make a colossal mistake."

Anita made coffee for herself.

"I'll make another one for Gabriele later. I admire your determination to keep working. Most women would just think of the baby and getting the nursery ready."

Rachele put the first layer of filling on the cake.

"This is my second child. Emma moved out of the cot a few months ago. I have already looked at Emma's baby clothes and I know what I need to replace, and the grandmothers are buying something new for the new one. I'll have time when I stop working in a couple of weeks."

Rachele took a deep breath, a reaction to the smell of coffee that was invading the kitchen.

"I miss the idea of coffee, but I am beginning to dislike the smell."

Anita took the coffee machine off the stove. They heard Emma cry.

"Anita, I am in the middle of baking. Do you mind getting Emma? I'll come as soon as the cake is in the oven."

On their way to work, Gabriele noticed he could not distract his wife from whatever had been on her mind.

"I thought you stopped going to court a couple of months ago."

They were waiting for the vaporetto. Rachele looked as if her husband's words had brought her back from whatever place she was in her mind.

"I am not going to court. Today Alvise, Dario and I will each talk to one person. I hope the outcome will allow me to present my theory to Antonio Penzo with enough information rather than with just a gut feeling."

The vaporetto had arrived, and Gabriele focused on finding a seat for his wife. He found two seats in the back, away from the rest of the passengers.

"Do you still think you have to impress Antonio Penzo?"

Rachele turned to him with a relaxed face. It was the first time he saw her relaxed that morning.

"I do. In the beginning, he thought I was an entitled spoiled young woman, but then he changed his mind. Now I consider him my litmus test if I am good at what I am doing."

Gabriele put an arm around his wife's shoulders

"You are good at what you do. So good that your boss has adjusted to your pregnancies, your extended family, and your leading a life under a different calendar."

When Laszlo Kron arrived at the offices of the Venier-Zanin law firm, the receptionist explained to him he might have to wait a few minutes for Rachele. She led the way into the meeting room, asked Mr Kron to sit down, and moved an armchair and a footstool to the opposite side of the table. She explained they were eager to keep Rachele as comfortable as possible in the last couple of weeks before she started her leave.

When Rachele walked into the room, she found her client so deep in thought that he had not noticed her arrival. He immediately stood up, greeted her, and sat down only after she did and reassured him she was comfortable.

"Mr Kron, thank you for coming. I hope you will excuse me if I come straight to the point. This could be a delicate conversation, something I felt had to be done person to person. How well do you know Gino Moras?"

The question surprised Laszlo Kron

"I asked the notary who supervised the sale of what is now Villa Kalman if he knew somebody who could take care of any paperwork associated with the house. My Italian is not good, I asked for somebody who could speak German. The notary introduced me to Gino Moras. It turned out he had a Hungarian wife. His Hungarian is better than my Italian."

"What else can you tell me about him?"

"I'm afraid there isn't much to tell. He has a set of keys and has taken care of any local tax I am supposed to pay. In the beginning, I gave him a deposit then at the end of each month he sends me the bills he has paid and I send him a cheque from my bank here in Venice. May I ask you why you ask these questions?"

Rachele was not comfortable discussing her theories unless she had some evidence. This time, her evidence was only the way Gino Moras behaved.

"Gino Moras mentioned his brother a lot. A brother that nobody has seen as yet. Each time I spoke to him, I got the impression there was something he was not disclosing or something he wanted to hide. Therefore, I grew curious about him. I have no evidence yet, but my instinct tells me there is something I need to investigate."

Laszlo Kron was silent for a few minutes. Rachele could almost see his mind trying to retrieve any memory.

"I have never heard of a brother. I know he has a brother-in-law who is a photographer here at the Lido."

"Would he be his Hungarian wife's brother?"

"I am not sure. Mario Dolfin may know more."

Rachele thanked him and moved on to discuss the reply she had received on the two contracts with theatre companies who wanted to stage the Italian version of two of the operettas for which Laszlo Kron's company had European rights. After her client left, and she was back in her office with her feet up, she rang Mario Dolfin. After a short preamble, she came straight to the point.

"I do not want to keep you. Laszlo Kron told me that Gino Moras has a brother-in-law who is a photographer at the Lido. Do you know whether he is Hungarian?"

Mario Dolfin's answer confirmed her gut feeling.

"There is a Hungarian photographer at the Lido. I do not know whether he is his brother-in-law."

"Thank you for your information. You have been very helpful."

Rachele opened her Villa Kalman notepad and went to the diagram she had drawn after reading Franz Donda's diary. She wrote 'Hungarian photographer, Lido, Dario Zago to investigate'. Half an hour later, Alvise Cantoni knocked at her door. He told her he had asked his contacts, and they did not know of any Moras who was a member of the banned Socialist party in Venice. Alvise added that his confidential contact would know. Rachele knew better than to ask for further details.

The third person she had to see before her meeting with Antonio Penzo arrived when she was still talking to Alvise. Dario Zago had spent the morning walking along the beach with Thomas Donda. He had convinced his mother and Mrs Kron that he would respect the exercise regimen the doctor had prescribed. Thomas had to sit down every twenty minutes, and Dario had to be careful not to tire him too much. They had a very interesting conversation. It turned out that the family had a system to communicate with Franz Donda, despite the war. Their mother had a sister working in Switzerland, they would send letters through her. In his last letter, Franz wrote he had met somebody who looked like the Hungarian army officer who lived down the road from them but he spoke Venetian dialect. That person had started talking to him whenever they met. Franz had kept up his cover. A medical student from a small town in North Eastern Italy near the border, on the Italian side. The person was asking too many questions, and Franz wondered if the entire operation had been compromised. Thomas remembered the Hungarian army officer whose family used to live near them in Gorizia or Görz, as the city was called in German. At that point, Dario Zago paused for effect, then continued.

"Thomas is sure that the man his brother described in the letter was the last person who saw him alive."

Rachele added.

"Or the person who killed his brother. Did Thomas tell you what happened to him before they found him in the shed?"

Dario took a deep breath.

"He only remembers walking towards the Grand Hotel Des Bains, then things become sketchy. He thinks he was talking to somebody he can't describe and does not remember how he ended up in the shed."

Alvise shook his head. Rachele put down the pen, looked ahead of her, and sighed.

"That is a shame. We may have to wait for his memory to come back before we find out what happened. Meanwhile, I have another task for you before sending you back to your studies. Laszlo Kron told me Gino Moras has a brother-in-law who is a photographer at the Lido. Mario Dolfin tells me that a Hungarian photographer is working at the Lido. Could you find out whether he is Gino Moras' brother-in-law?"

Franco Venier told Rachele he had an arrangement with Antonio Penzo to have drinks after their meeting. So she did not expect him before 4pm. He arrived very early when she had one of the Italian theatres who was negotiating a contract with Mr Kron on the phone.

Fifteen minutes later, she walked into the meeting room, followed by Alvise Cantoni. She apologised to keep him waiting, but the magistrate had arrived earlier than expected. Antonio Penzo looked excited. It turned out he had something to contribute to the conversation.

"I am early because I went on a wild goose chase and found something. Isacco Bloch had reported the disappearance of Franz Donda. In his report to the police, he defined him as exiled from the 'unredeemed land of Gorizia', but he reported him. We have his description and a photo."

Rachele and Alvise looked at the photo and looked at each other. Alvise went back to Rachele's office and collected the bag with the diary and Franz's documents. When he re-joined them, Rachele took out the Austrian travel document and showed it to Antonio Penzo.

"Probably the photograph you had comes from here. This is the travel document issued by the Austrian Empire to young men who had to travel abroad despite not having completed, or started, their military service."

Antonio Penzo looked at the photo. The quarter of the official stamp in the photo matched the three quarters still left in the document.

Rachele exposed her theory to the magistrate. Thomas' memory loss was also a problem, but she thought they were following the right set of clues. Antonio Penzo needed to be convinced.

"Are you sure the disappearance of Franz Donda, and his brother Thomas being battered to the point of spending a week in a coma, are connected?"

Rachele was ready.

"Thomas itself told me he had come to Venice to find out what happened to his brother. His parents paid for an empty grave at the cemetery. Connecting the disappearance and the beatings is a legitimate assumption."

Antonio Penzo had learnt that he could trust this young woman who had elbowed her way into a male professional world and thrived.

"Where would the evidence be?"

Rachele thought about it for a few minutes, looked at Alvise, then said.

"I think Gino Moras is the key. He knows more than what he shared with us. Each time he talked to me, he was vague enough to raise more than one alarm bell. He is our starting point in proving the connection."

Alvise had an idea

"We could think of a way to bring Gino Moras and Thomas Donda together and see what happens."

The magistrate, Rachele, and Franco Venier did not have the time to answer or make suggestions. The receptionist knocked at the door and walked in.

"Avvocato Modiano, I have Laszlo Kron on the phone. He says it is very urgent."

Rachele walked out of the meeting room and picked up the call on one of the secretary's desk.

"Mr Kron, how can I help?"

"Please call the police for me and send somebody here from your law firm as well. My wife, my children, and I have just come back from afternoon tea at the Excelsior with friends. When we came back, I realised I did not take the key to the front door, so we went to the back entrance. The back door was open. We found our housekeeper unconscious on the floor and the door to the basement was open. The strange thing is that Thomas Donda was in his room with Dario Zago and his mother, and they heard nothing."

"How is the housekeeper?"

"Dario Zago's mother ran to our neighbours, the retired local midwife, for help. Mrs Volpato is looking after her at the moment. She also called a doctor."

"Did you touch anything in the basement?"

"I did not. I remembered Dario Zago's attitude when we forced the basement door open, so I did not go in or touch the door. We found the door open and the light on."

"Perfect. Tell Dario Zago to call the police. I trust him, but his German is not great. Maybe ask Mario Dolfin for help if he can send one of his staff who speaks German. I trust Dario. I also think that whoever did it does not know the existence of the hidden changing rooms and wants to find what we have found already. He did not find it in the shed. He is looking for it in the basement."

Rachele went back to the meeting room. She sat down and simply said.

"I think we have an unexpected help. Somebody is probably looking for what we found. They could not find it in the shed, and they are now looking in the basement. There has been a break-in at Villa Kalman. They ransacked the basement. Dario Zago is there, he will call the police."

Chapter Fourteen

January 1926

6 January 1926

Gabriele and Rachele were proud to be Jewish. January 6th, the Epiphany, was a Christian holiday and the Mendes household used to ignore it. However, since Emma was born, they had decided that there was nothing wrong in keeping the Italian tradition of the legendary old lady, the *Befana*, bringing gifts to children during the night flying on her broom. So Emma found toys by the kitchen windowsill when she woke up for breakfast. The grown-ups around her did not specifically mention the Befana, but they all acted surprised to find a parcel with Emma's name on the windowsill.

January 6th was a national holiday. Anita walked into the kitchen with another parcel for Emma, claiming that the Befana had left something on her windowsill by mistake. Emma was too busy for breakfast. The phone interrupted that happy family moment. Rachele took the call.

"Good morning Rachele, I am sorry to bother you on a holiday, but I wonder if we can talk while things are still fresh in my mind."

"Good morning Mr Kron. How are you? It is not a problem."

Anita stopped helping Gabriele convince Emma that breakfast was better than her new toys and brought a chair near the phone so Rachele could sit down.

"I just wanted to say that Dario Zago has been brilliant. He insisted the police took fingerprints of anything that was likely to have been touched or moved. He thought they were clearly after what we had found in the hidden changing rooms."

"I know I could count on him. He is going to be a brilliant lawyer. How is your housekeeper?"

"According to Mrs Volpato, they kept her in hospital for observation. She will probably stay until tomorrow morning."

"I think they might be worried she has a concussion. It is a good sign. It means they did not cause her any major harm."

"Dario thinks we should not leave Thomas Donda alone. So he has organised my wife, his mother, and one of his siblings to take turns being with him today. He also asked me to tell you he will come to your office tomorrow to give you a full report. I may come with him."

"I think I only have one meeting tomorrow, in the morning. If you come in the afternoon, I am free. When are you going back to Vienna?"

"My family leaves Sunday night. I am going to Milan on Tuesday, back on Thursday, and then I shall travel to Vienna the following Saturday night."

The conversation ended after Rachele invited the Krons for lunch after synagogue.

7 January 1926

Dario Zago told Laszlo Kron he had errands to run and would meet him at the law firm. He wanted to discuss something he had planned to do with Rachele alone. So he arrived in the morning with a book. It was not the first time he used an empty meeting room or an empty desk to study while waiting for Rachele or her boss to be available. He was concentrating on his textbook on criminal law when Rachele coughed to announce her presence.

"I can't say I remember that book with pleasure, but I remember it. Why did you want to see me alone? Follow me to my office so I can put my feet up."

Dario closed the book, stood up, and followed her to her office. On the way, Rachele asked a secretary to see if Alvise was free to join them in her office. Once Alvise joined them, Dario could start.

"The other day, you were explaining to Alvise and me your gut feeling about Gino Moras. When you asked me to check if the photographer at the Lido was Hungarian, I wondered if there was a legal way I could get his fingerprints. Then it came to me on my way home, so I paid a visit to my father's office at the Excelsior and I asked him and Mario Dolfin if they had a roll of film to process."

Rachele and Alvise looked at each other, then they both looked at Dario, their faces revealing their approval.

"I thought he was unlikely to have employees in the winter. When he handed me an envelope with the photographs and asked me to check if they were my photos, I asked him if he minded taking them out because I was wearing gloves. So the first two photos in the envelope had his fingerprints."

Rachele looked at him again

"That is a brilliant idea. Where are the photos now?"

"I took them to the police station and asked them to be dusted for prints. I might have mentioned your name and told them you asked me to do it and if they had any problem, they could check with your magistrate friend, Antonio Penzo."

Rachele decided there and then to tell Franco Venier they should give him a permanent job before another law firm took him from them.

"Antonio Penzo is not my friend. He is a friend of my boss, Avvocato Venier. Other than that, well done! We shall know if my gut feeling was right, or in the right direction."

Dario was pleased with himself. He had another question before going back to his book, waiting for Laszlo Kron.

"I am curious. Can you share your gut feeling with us?"

Rachele noticed Alvise had a huge grin on his face.

"Alvise smiles because my husband always tells me to talk from Chapter 1 instead of starting the conversation in my head and then open my mouth when I reach Chapter 4. My theory is that Gino Moras, or his brother-in-law, or both of them were spies. Somehow Franz found out, and they had to stop him from revealing their identity to the authorities."

Alvise was looking at his notes.

"That is plausible. How does Franz's brother, Thomas, get in the picture?"

"Thomas Donda must have known, or found out, that his brother kept a diary. So he thought the diary held the key to his death. Those who killed him thought the diary held the key to Franz figuring out they were spies, or he was a spy. Thomas must have contacted one of them, without knowing their past."

Dario apologised before interrupting

"Thomas only wanted to find out what happened to his brother."

"Yes, but he knew about the existence of a diary. They could not know what was in the diary, so they might have helped Thomas hoping to find the diary. They knew it was not in the basement, because they had been there already. That is why they took him to the shed after they beat him up or where they beat him up."

～

Rachele did not expect to see Thomas Donda with Laszlo Kron. The afternoon was proving more interesting than she expected. She asked the receptionist to contact Dario Zago and Alvise, asking them to join Rachele and the visitors in the meeting room. When they entered the room, they interrupted a conversation in German. It turned out Thomas was fluent in German as well.

The moment Thomas noticed Alvise and Dario, he apologised to Laszlo Kron, then switched to Italian.

"Yesterday afternoon, something Dario's mother asked me to translate for Mrs Kron brought an image to my mind; I realised that my memory was coming back."

A couple of days earlier, Thomas was sitting on a bench reading one of his brother's letters. Their mother kept them all. Somebody sat next to him and they started talking. He asked the stranger if he was from the Lido, because he had a description of the place where his brother was staying during the early years of the war and hadn't found it yet. The stranger listened to the description. He thought he recognised it, but he was not in Venice ten years earlier. His brother-in-law was. Thomas asked him how he could talk to the stranger's brother-in-law, and the stranger said he would talk to his brother-in-law and if Thomas told him where he was staying he would let him know where and when he could meet his brother-in-law. Thomas finished the tale by saying,

130

"I only remember I agreed to meet somebody after work outside the Grand Hotel Des Bains. The rest has not come back to me yet."

Laszlo Kron had already heard the tale. He turned to Rachele.

"Given our conversation a couple of days ago, I am sure you and I thought of the same person."

Alvise, who spoke some German added, in Italian.

"I think Dario and I thought of the same person as well."

Rachele turned to Thomas Donda

"Does the name Gino Moras mean anything to you?"

"It does not, should it?"

"No, not necessarily, but don't be surprised if we introduced you to him."

She then turned to Laszlo Kron and said in German,

"What happens when you are not in Venice?"

Laszlo Kron had already discussed it with Thomas and Dario

"When I leave, Dario moves in. This time, he will stay in one of the guest rooms, probably near Thomas. He needs to be at the Hospital for the last check at the end of next week. His energy is coming back. I have arranged with Mario Dolfin that, when Dario is not in, he spends his time at the Hotel Excelsior with a book."

Rachele turned to the others.

"I need to share this conversation with Antonio Penzo. Thanks to Dario, we may not need to wait until Thomas recovers his memory. If he recognised Gino Moras, we can leave the rest to the police."

She then turned to Laszlo Kron in German

"Can you organise a meeting at Villa Kalman on Monday afternoon? I'll take a water taxi and will also try to see if a senior magistrate and a policeman could be there. I want to put Thomas and Gino Moras in the same room and see what happens."

~

Rachele reckoned she was about five weeks from giving birth. It was unusual for a woman to flaunt her pregnancy at that stage, but she did not care. Gabriele had to work late, so he had organised the cavalry to walk Rachele home. When she was about to leave, she found her mother-in-law, Fiamma, and her aunt, Countess Deborah, ready to escort her home. She missed her husband, but she enjoyed the company. The first thing the countess did was to point out to her childhood friend how smart Rachele looked in the maternity dress she had organised. Rachele thought that her aunt Deborah could not have sounded more proud if she had put together the dress herself. When they boarded the vaporetto, the countess asked a young man to give up his seat for her niece. Rachele felt very self-conscious during the exchange, but knew she needed to sit.

On the way, the conversation was all about the social arrangements for the Sabbath meals. It was Countess Pesaro De Bonfili's turn to have both families. Rachele tried to say that she was looking forward to spending her day with her feet up and would send Gabriele and Emma to represent her household. She had already organised a relaxed Sunday with her friend Sofia Mondani, Gabriele and Paolo would take Arrigo and Emma out. The journey home ended with no major breach of family diplomatic relationships. When the two friends delivered her home, they chatted with Anita for a while. She told them that Rachele was getting very tired at the end of the day, much more than when she was expecting Emma. They had not discussed the weekend yet, but Rachele planned to spend it with her feet up before starting her last week at work before her three months' leave.

The two childhood friends declined Anita's offer to stay for dinner and left. Anita went to see if Rachele needed anything and found her in the sitting room. She had taken her shoes off, was sitting on an armchair with her feet on the coffee table.

"Do you need a cushion for your feet?"

"Thank you Anita, I am fine. May I ask what you talked about with Fiamma and Aunt Deborah?"

Anita picked up Emma from the playpen and sat her on her small armchair next to her mother with a book

"I told them you were looking forward to a day where you could put your feet up, but Gabriele and Emma would join them."

"Thank you."

Emma started saying something with a tune she had made up. Rachele tried to understand what Emma was trying to mimic. Anita had an idea.

"This afternoon Fiamma asked me to help her with her meat shopping. She volunteered Roberto to baby-sit. Emma loves spending time with her youngest uncle. Roberto was studying for his bar-mitzvah.[1] I think she tries to mimic him."

A few seconds later, Rachele could hear her daughter saying 'iiissshhh tzaaaadiiiiik' then continuing blabbering something, trying to mimic her uncle's chanting.

"I see Roberto hasn't gone very far. If I remember correctly, those two words appear at the very beginning of the piece he is supposed to read. It says that Noah was a wise man."

Anita looked at Emma with pride.

"She may be two next month, but she listens when she is interested in something or curious about something."

Rachele added

"And there are few things that Emma finds more interesting than her uncle Roberto, her cousin Carlo, her honorary cousin Arrigo or her father."

They heard Gabriele open the door and come in. Emma stood up and ran towards her father, who picked her up and lifted her above his head with a huge grin. Emma laughed and looked at her father in a way that showed that, at the moment, there was nobody else in the world.

Gabriele put her down and asked her to take him to see mummy. Emma went back to her chair at a leisurely pace, set down and re-started her game. Rachele felt compelled to explain that Roberto was babysitting in the afternoon.

Chapter Fifteen

January 1926

11 January 1926

It was the first day of the last week of going to the office before Rachele's three-month leave. Rachele hoped they would sort out what happened at Villa Kalman before the end of the week.

In the years following her first meeting with Antonio Penzo, the magistrate had got used to the idea of a woman being a competent professional. He had stopped using a patronising tone. However, he was not sure what to do when he was around a heavily pregnant woman in a professional context. Rachele could sense that he wanted to ask whether she was all right, but he thought it might annoy her after the first time. They both had news to report to the other. He had said ladies' first with a smile, but Rachele replied he was the guest, so he had precedence.

"We have matched fingerprints we found on the door handle with the ones that were found in the rifle that shot at those two teenagers last September."

Rachele almost stood up in triumph, except she didn't because these days it took a while for her to get up.

"And I remember the locksmith changed the handle when he forced the door open so the fingerprints are recent."

"Indeed, we also found the same set of fingerprints in two places in the basement. We do not have the results of the Hungarian photographer's fingerprints. By the way, the police praised the way Dario Zago's got them."

Now it was Rachele's turn to share an interesting development. She updated the magistrate about Thomas Donda, remembering something that happened before they found him in the shed.

"Following my gut feeling, Laszlo Kron has arranged for Gino Moras to come to the Villa this afternoon. If Thomas Donda recognises him, we have evidence that may indicate that Gino Moras' brother-in-law met him. Alvise Cantoni is talking to the police at the Lido to arrange for a plainclothes agent to be present. If things go according to my theory, we move from acting on my gut feeling to acting on circumstantial evidence."

Antonio Penzo couldn't help himself.

"Although it wouldn't be the first time that acting on your gut feeling led to us finding evidence."

Rachele appreciated further evidence that his original condescending tone had gone; she patted her belly

"Although these days this baby is squeezing my guts, so they may not be as reliable as they usually are."

Antonio Penzo did not know how to react to that. Alvise Cantoni saved him when he joined them.

"The police agreed to have a plainclothes man at this afternoon's meeting. They also told me they may have processed the fingerprints in the envelope by then."

Antonio Penzo felt he was back on solid ground.

"If they match, that would put the photographer at the Villa last Tuesday evening. Even if we do not have the result, someone may just hint at it to see how Gino Moras reacts."

Rachele did not like quashing the magistrate's enthusiasm, but she had to say it

"Although, without the fingerprints, a good lawyer could destroy your case in court."

Antonio Penzo laughed and turned to her

"So, you'd better not take this case, or advise the lawyer who takes this case."

When Gabriele introduced Rachele to his childhood friend Paolo Mondani and his wife Sofia, there was an instant rapport between them. Since then, the bond between the two couples had grown closer and closer. Paolo and Sofia had bought separate pots, pans, plates, and cutlery so they could have their friends for a meal that would follow Jewish dietary rules. Sofia had issued a standing invitation for lunch for the entire week. They lived near the Rialto fish market, very close to Rachele's office. Rachele was delighted to accept it would have allowed her time to keep her feet up after lunch. Sofia also invited Anita and Emma, so Gabriele and Rachele could still see their daughter during their lunch break.

Sofia and Anita insisted Rachele had a rest on the sofa. She did not realise she had fallen asleep. When she opened her eyes, she saw Arrigo reading to Emma, who was listening with a huge grin on her face. Gabriele came to tell her it was time to get up. They had to meet the taxi arranged by Laszlo Kron at the agreed spot near the Rialto bridge. Rachele thanked Sofia for her hospitality and Anita for bringing Emma. Hugged them, kissed Emma and Arrigo and left with Gabriele and Paolo. They crossed the Rialto bridge and met

Alvise. Gabriele left for work, Paolo hitched a ride to the Lido. It was his first shift as a doctor at the hospital where he had been an emergency nurse until a month earlier.

~

On their way to the Lido, Rachele felt queasy for the first time. Paolo looked at her and asked the driver to slow down a bit. When they arrived at the pier opposite the Hotel Excelsior, they found Laszlo Kron waiting for them.

"I was getting anxious waiting for you. I never felt this nervous on an opening night. Let's hope this is the last of the Villa Kalman's secrets."

Rachele accepted his hand to steady herself as she was getting off the water taxi.

"We'll soon find out whether my guts were wrong."

It was a short walk to the Villa and when they arrived; the plainclothes policeman introduced himself and told them they had processed the fingerprints in the envelope and they matched. The news put Alvise and Rachele in a good mood. When they walked into the sitting room, they found Dario Zago and Thomas Donda sorting out chairs. Rachele was almost euphoric.

"Dario, your ploy worked. The fingerprints match! The photographer was here last Tuesday night and was also the one who shot at the two teenagers!"

Thomas Donda applauded, and Dario took a bow. The bell rang; the two young men and the policeman moved into the adjacent room. They had agreed to a specific order in which they would enter the sitting room. The policeman was going to join them only when they summoned him.

When Laszlo Kron entered the room with Gino Moras, Rachele was sitting in one of the armchairs. She stood up to greet him. Gino Moras looked confused. Laszlo Kron tried to be reassuring.

"Avvocato Modiano is here because we have a separate business to deal with today and can help me if my Italian is not good enough."

Gino Moras was still confused.

"But I am fluent in German."

Laszlo Kron tried to be as reassuring as possible

"I know that, but Dario Zago is not, and he will join us in a few minutes."

It was time for Rachele to say what they had agreed before the weekend.

"I am here to discuss a separate legal matter with Mr Kron, but members of the family who sold the house to Mr Kron has asked me to find out something they only have come across when they looked inside a trunk they took from here when they emptied the house. By any chance, does the name Marasich mean anything to you?"

Gino Moras' reaction convinced Rachele she was moving in the right direction. He seemed to sink deeper into the armchair.

"Not really, should it?"

"I do not know, the name features in the last entry of the diary of a young man who disappeared in 1916. The Bloch family would like to find out what happened to him."

Laszlo Kron excused himself. His wife was already in Vienna. He had to check how long it would take for refreshments to be served. It was part of the plan. Gino Moras switched to Italian,

"Why should I know a Mr Marasich?"

Rachele got up, opened the door to the dining room, and sat down again.

"I am not sure, except I think you have some knowledge of Franz Donda and what happened to him."

Gino Moras looked defeated. His look turned into positive fear when he saw Thomas Donda entering the room followed by Alvise Cantoni and Dario Zago. He stood up, trying to leave, but Laszlo Kron was faster and blocked the door.

"I do not think you should go. There is the police outside that door ready to stop you. This is your last chance to have some help."

Gino Moras almost fell back. He landed on the armchair where he had been sitting earlier.

"How did you know?"

Rachele apologised to Alvise and Dario in Italian. They knew the story anyway.

"I did not. You were always vague when you were talking to me; you always appeared at the right time or had mentioned a brother than nobody ever saw. I started being suspicious when a reliable and confidential source told me that the banned Socialist party in Venice did not have a Moras amongst his members."

Rachele noticed that Thomas Donda was translating for her colleagues, so she slowed the pace of her speech.

"It is very difficult to keep a secret in Venice. It is a very small place. The Lido is even smaller. We found out you have a Hungarian wife and your brother-in-law is a photographer here at the Lido. We found Franz Donda's diary. The last entry mentions that he was about to meet a Mr Marasich."

Gino Moras interrupted Rachele.

"Where did you find it?"

Rachele hid her irritation.

"Anyway, acting on my gut feeling, I asked Dario to find out more about the Hungarian photographer in the Lido. He had the brilliant idea of getting his fingerprint legally without him being aware of it."

Rachele paused, almost as if she were confronting an uncooperative witness in court.

"We have found out this morning that the fingerprints match the ones found on the rifle used to shoot at the two teenagers who jumped the fence to retrieve the ball last September. They also match the fingerprints found on the door handle and other places in the basement following the recent break-in. Now, before I answer your questions, I need to ask Thomas Donda a question in Italian."

After another pause, Rachele switched to Italian.

"I need to ask you formally, so Alvise and Dario can testify. Thomas Donda, do you recognise the man who sat on the bench next to you two days before somebody beat you unconscious?"

Thomas Donda made a point of looking at Gino Moras.

"He never introduced himself, but he is in this room sitting opposite you. Today I found out that his name is Gino Moras."

Rachele thanked Thomas and continued,

"The police have enough information to charge your brother-in-law with breaking and entering, use of a rifle without a licence, we checked, and circumstantial evidence to charge him of causing grievous bodily harm to Thomas Donda. There is enough circumstantial evidence to charge you as an accomplice."

Gino Moras covered his face with his hands. Rachele stood up and used a more maternal tone. She switched to German.

"It may help you if you tell us what happened. It will also give Thomas peace of mind to know what happened to his brother. Did your brother-in-law kill him?"

Gino Moras looked at Rachele, then looked at Thomas.

"No, he did not. When Italy entered the war against the Austrian Empire, I hid the fact that I had a Hungarian wife and that her brother was living with us. Janos, my brother-in-law, was 18 in 1915. Mr Marasich was an Austrian agent who somehow found out about it and blackmailed us. Janos worked for him to stop the blackmail."

Laszlo Kron couldn't stay quiet any longer

"Why were you so eager to find the diary?"

Gino Moras ignores the question and continued

"I do not know how Janos met Franz Donda, but he gained his trust and introduced him to Mr Marasich. As far as we know, Mr Marasich abducted Franz, who must have died in prison or while they questioned him. I am not sure, but he left Venice alive. We were hoping to find the diary to see if there is any indication that Janos was linked with Mr Marasich."

"Why was it important?"

"We hoped that if there was no written evidence of Janos' activities, he could apply for citizenship."

Rachele felt she had to explain the legal issue to Laszlo Kron.

"They would not have approved his citizenship application if it had come out that he was aiding and abetting the enemy during the war."

Alvise had understood some of the conversation, enough to ask the question.

"Why beating up Thomas Donda?"

Gino Moras switched to Italian.

"I know it is difficult to prove, but Janos told me he did not. Thomas Donda was fine when they parted company."

They turned to Thomas, who looked lost.

"This is where I have no memory yet. I vaguely remember meeting somebody, but not what happened between the time I met him and when I woke up in hospital."

Dario Zago had an idea

"Has your coat been cleaned?"

Rachele and Alvise looked at each other, their faces lit up. Thomas thought about it for a while.

"I don't know where it is. When I left the hospital, your mother lent me some of your clothes and the ambulance that brought me here had used blankets to make sure I was warm enough. Mr Kron insisted on lending me one of his coats."

Rachele turned to Laszlo Kron in German

"if Mr Donda's coat is still in the shed, we can take it to the police and ask if they find fingerprints that do not belong to him. It could be a way to clear Gino Moras's brother-in-law or prove that he did it."

She then turned to Dario.

"Dario, ask the policeman in the other room to go to the shed with you and look for the coat."

Rachele felt very much like a big lady who was ordering people around because she couldn't move very well herself. Alvise was explaining to Gino Moras that he had better not move. Given what they have established so far, his brother-in-law shot at two teenagers and that, in itself, was a police matter. He was still chargeable with aiding and abetting a person who had committed something illegal.

Dario Zago and the policeman came back with the coat. The phone rang. The housekeeper came to tell Mr Kron it was the police. Mr Kron asked Alvise to take the call. He did not trust his Italian. When Alvise came back, he spoke to Gino Moras first, Thomas Donda was translating for Laszlo Kron.

"The police said that your brother-in-law is there, and I am supposed to tell the agent that is here that a car is coming for you and him, and he should take the coat to be examined, now that they found it."

Chapter Sixteen

January-February 1926

14 January 1926

Rachele only had two days at work before her three months' leave. She had little left to hand over to Alvise and only had two contracts left to sort out. She thought of taking them home and finishing the review at leisure. They were only due at the end of the month. Alvise would take the meeting with the client. She was briefing him when the receptionist came to announce that there was an unscheduled but urgent visit. Antonio Penzo had just arrived and said it was important. Avvocato Venier was with him in the large meeting room.

Rachele and Alvise looked at each other, shrugged their shoulders, picked up their notepad, and got up. When Rachele walked into the meeting room, Antonio Penzo and Franco Venier stood up. Franco Venier excused himself and left. Antonio Penzo had a smile and an apology.

"Early this week, I thought I would come today with a gift for the new child. I remember doing it for Emma, so I wanted to do it for this one. However, yesterday we had the results of the fingerprints found on the coat, and I wanted to run them past you to see if you have any brilliant idea of how to proceed."

Rachele adjusted herself on the armchair that had become her seat when she was in a meeting.

"Thank you for your gift. What did they find?"

Antonio Penzo sighed and took out a small notepad, opened it and started reading it.

"They found the same fingerprints on the back of the collar, and on one sleeve. Somebody grabbed Thomas Donda by the collar and, later, by the arm to drag him to the house. They found the same print somewhere else in the shed. Based on the fingerprint, they think Thomas Donda was not beaten up in the shed but was forced to walk to the shed. He probably fainted later when his attacker left."

Rachele hoped she could take the image out of her mind. She had to. She should think like a lawyer, not like a mother. Alvise looked at her and asked the question.

"Did the police identify anybody from those fingerprints?"

Antonio Penzo sighed again.

"We have definitely excluded Gino Moras and his brother-in-law, Janos Horvath. I am here to pick your brain about who else can it be?"

Rachele closed her eyes, her hands joined with the two index fingers sticking out and touching her lips. Alvise mouthed "She is thinking" to Antonio Penzo, who nodded. After a while, she opened her eyes and straightened up.

"This may be a long shot, but when Gino Moras appeared right after the housekeeper found Thomas Donda in the shed, he said that the foreman of the team working at Villa Kalman contacted him. He could be a possibility. Mario Dolfin, the manager of Hotel Excelsior, has the contact details of Mr Kron's housekeeper. Between the two of them, they may know how to contact the foreman."

Antonio Penzo finished writing on his notepad.

"Thank you. That is as good a suggestion as any. As you said, it may be a long shot, but it is the only lead we may have. I'll let Franco know how it ends. Meanwhile, take care of yourself and let me know whether it is a boy or a girl."

He stood up, told Rachele not to stand up on his account, thanked them for their time, and left. Alvise saw him to the door, then joined Rachele in her office.

"What is the likelihood of Mr Marasich re-appearing in Venice?"

Rachele was looking inside a drawer. She looked up.

"What makes you say that?"

"Who else other than Gino Moras and his brother-in-law had any interest in the diary or in stopping Thomas Donda from finding out about his brother?"

26 January 1926

Rachele did not like being idle. There was only so much time she could spend with her feet up reading a book before boredom set in. Everybody around her wanted her to relax, and rest until the new baby arrived. Her restlessness was obvious to Anita, who had secretly organised women in the overall Mendes clan to come and keep her busy. That day it was Sofia Mondani's turn. The weather was nice, so they sat outside in the Campo watching Arrigo and Emma play. Rachele could manage small talk only for a short time, but her friend could get a piece of granite to talk, so the conversation was flowing. Rachele was watching Arrigo playing with Emma.

"He is very protective. He is also very good at following Emma, but making sure she doesn't go too far away from us."

Sofia was about to reply when she noticed Alvise Cantoni and two young men approach from Calle del Tentor.

"I think you have visitors. Alvise and two young men are walking towards us. If they need to talk to you about work, I'll take care of Emma. We all come up."

Sofia called Arrigo who got hold of Emma and, holding her hand, started walking towards her. They greeted Alvise, who was with Dario Zago and Thomas Donda. Sofia suggested that the two young men grab one chair each, and they all climbed the two flights of steps.

Once they were inside, Anita and Sofia guided the children to the kitchen with the promise of hot chocolate and biscuits. Rachele took the visitors to the sitting room. Once they were all sitting down, Alvise sort of took over.

"We are here because Thomas goes back home tomorrow, and he wanted to come and say goodbye and thank you. We also have some recent developments to share with you."

Anita appeared with biscuits

"What would you like to drink? We can only provide tea or hot chocolate. Rachele reacts badly even to the smell of coffee these days. Gabriele and I go to a nearby café for our morning coffee."

Once Anita left, Thomas thanked her for her help. He was very grateful to her, Alvise, the Zago family and the Kron family for all the help they had provided. Laszlo Kron also offered him a job for a project he had in mind starting in the summer when he was in Venice and had time to set up operations in Italy. Rachele was intrigued and was sure that she would find out in due course. After Anita came with the teas and hot chocolates, Alvise felt he could share the recent developments.

"Antonio Penzo wants to know if you have some magic powers. You were right. The foreman was working under an assumed name. Even Marasich was an assumed name. His real name is Bruno Walther, the son of an officer in the Austrian army from Graz and an Italian woman from Gorizia."

Rachele was lying on the sofa.

"It wasn't even a gut feeling. It was the only person I could think of. Why was he in Venice now?"

Thomas was faster than Alvise

"He was after my brother's diary. Janos was not the only one who was afraid of the past. Except he wanted to clean up his past to rise in the hierarchy of the Fascist Party. He thought I knew where it was hidden."

"And did you?"

Thomas shook his head.

"The only thing I knew was that Franz was working behind the garden shed. Bruno thought I did not want to share it. I still have no memory of the beating, and I do not know how I ended up in the shed. Anyway, it is not important, he confessed."

Dario Zago had something else to share

"I now have a full-time job with the law firm. I am your researcher."

Alvise added

"And he has impressed the police and Antonio Penzo. They suggested he contacts them after he graduates."

They stayed and chatted for about an hour until Sofia knocked at the door to say that she and Arrigo were leaving. Arrigo walked in, hugged Rachele and, with a very adult tone of voice, told her to take care of his new cousin. He said goodbye to Alvise and shook hands with Dario and Thomas. Sofia looked at her son, then looked at Rachele, and they both smiled.

13 February 1926

Rachele had stopped going to synagogue. She was getting closer to her due date and did not want to risk starting labour during service. She and Gabriele had organised lunch after the synagogue service. They had invited their friends Paolo and Sofia Mondani with their son Arrigo, and Alvise and Viola Cantoni with their son Franco. The Mondanis were not Jewish, so they had volunteered to show up early to help. Gabriele's baby brother, Roberto, had insisted on joining them.

Rachele had enjoyed lunch. She was getting up to go with Anita to fetch the cake when she immediately sat back. Sofia and Viola looked at each other, then looked at Rachele. Anita decided she had a surprise for the children in the kitchen. Gabriele looked at Paolo, who told him to call the midwife. Gabriele decided to send Roberto and gave him directions to her home. Meanwhile, Paolo was walking Rachele to her bedroom.

01 March 1926

Alvise had informed the law firm and a few other people. Mario Dolfin had organised a water taxi to take the Mendeses and Anita to the entrance of the Ghetto the morning of the baby naming ceremony. Despite the early hour of a Monday morning, the Mendes clan was in synagogue, including the Mondanis and the Cantonis. Rachele's parents had arrived from Trieste. Franco Venier was there as well. The ceremony followed the tradition of many Italian Jews. Anita was holding Emma, who had fallen asleep at the most important moment of the ceremony. Rachele was holding the baby.

Gabriele was called to the reading of the law; Rachele gave the baby to Countess Pesaro De Bonfili, who had the task of carrying the two-week-old girl to her father. She started walking down the stairs from the women's gallery and stopped at the top of the stairs into the men's section of the Spanish synagogue. On his way to the Tevah,[1] Gabriele took his new daughter from the arms of his aunt. At the end of the reading, after he said the blessing, the Rabbi recited the blessing for a newborn girl. He then stopped and asked Gabriele the name of his daughter. Fighting tears, Gabriele said the name following the tradition of Western Sephardi Jews 'Hannah Esther de Gabriel Mendes'. He also added that she was to be known as Anna Mendes.

Acknowledgments

I'll never tire of repeating it. Writing may be a solitary endeavour but it takes a village to create a book. Let me start by thanking my beta readers Rose Kemps, Andrea Rosen, Patricia Lane, Patricia Wallace, and Barbara Poll. Their feedback has been invaluable. You owe it to them if you do not fall asleep reading this book!

The London Writers' Salon (LWS) makes writing less solitary. You are one of several squares on a Zoom screen up to four times a day (so far). We all write "alone but together". It's magic. Try it if you do not believe it. London Writers' Salon is also a source of friends who provide encouragement and, by talking about our books, we bounce ideas from each other. The Gold coaches Kathryn, Niamh, Eimar, and Anna support you and help you get unstuck or recover your motivation on bad days. Fellow gold members are a group of cheerleaders who support you and cheer you. Whether the journey has been long or short, I would not have been able to do it without them.

A separate thank-you to Tracy Bickley who inspired me to get on with it without waiting for an agent. Four books and a collection of short stories later, I am very happy I did.

Family and friends provided encouragement, and listened (or acted as if they listened) when I let off steam, when I bragged, and when I bored them. Thank you Alessandra, Alessandro, Maria Vittoria, David, Michelle, Eyal, Moshe, Jonathan, and Sam.

I am also grateful to the librarian of the Biblioteca Marciana in Venice, who helped me (with a straight face) when I was trying to find sources of information about life in Venice in 1925 and 1926. I was not born then and most of the people who were are no longer with us.

Last but not least, thank you Venice. It is a city vilified by over-tourism, but the magic is still there. If you move away from Instagram locations and the hordes of visitors, you can still find magical corners. Writing stories that take place in Venice takes me back there and makes me relive the magic from the comfort of my home in London, by the river Thames.

Notes

Chapter 2

1. In 1925, legal adulthood started after the 21st birthday.

Chapter 5

1. A Kipferl is a vanilla-flavoured crescent shaped shortbread biscuit. The recipe originated in Austria.
2. Vaporetto (lit. little – or cute - steam engine) is the name Venetian use to indicate the waterbus.
3. Lungomare (lit. along the sea) is the name Italians give to an urban road that follows the coastline. Usually a wide road with trees and benches, what the French call *corniche*. *Lungomare Malamocco* changed name after WWII, it is now called *Lungomare Guglielmo Marconi*
4. In Judaism, the Sabbath starts at Sunset on Friday night and lasts about 25 hours.

Chapter 6

1. The Italian Social Democracy party was formed in 1922 as a merger of smaller centre-left parties that did not have a republican or a far left political idea. The party was one of those banned by Mussolini in 1926.
2. Rosh HaShanah (literally Head of the Year), the Jewish New Year. In 1925 it fell on September 19th and September 20th. Gabriele is telling Rachele he had known for a couple of months.

Chapter 8

1. After world war I, Bela Kun led a government that aligned itself with the Soviet union. The Hungarian Soviet Republic lasted until a counterrevolution put in place a new government in 1920, the new government tried to restore the Habsburg monarchy.
2. Cars are allowed in the Lido.

Chapter 9

1. In Italy in 1925 a first degree in law was at least four academic years.
2. One of the *sestieri*, the six administrative areas of the old city of Venice

Chapter 10

1. Franz Ferdinand Habsburg was the heir to the throne of the Austrian Empire and the kingdom of Hungary. His assassination in Sarajevo in June 1914 was the sparkle that triggered World War I.
2. In 1914 two of Rachele's brother travelled from Trieste, in those days the main port of the Austrian Empire, to Italy via Greece to join the Italian army and fight for Italy with the hope that the Italian speaking territories of the Empire would join Italy after the war (this is mentioned in the book "The Dressmaker's Parcels", available on Amazon.
3. At the onset of the twentieth century, there were Italian speaking areas in the Austrian empire, Italian nationalist were calling for the 'redemption' of these areas which were collectively called 'unredeemed lands'
4. In Judaism, a day starts at sunset. Therefore, the Sabbath goes from sunset Friday to nightfall Saturday. In December days are shorts and Rachele would have needed to be home at least an hour before Shabbat to be changed and ready to light the candles and 'usher Shabat in' in her home.

Chapter 11

1. Nazario Sauro really existed, one of the many Italian subjects of the Austrian empire who fought for Italy in World War I rather than against Italy. He was born in Capodistria, near Trieste. A city that is now in Slovenia but used to be part of Italy between World War I and World War II.
2. Adriatic club

Chapter 12

1. The original name for *Ghetto Nuovo* (new ghetto) was *'geto novo'*, in Venetian Dialect new bell foundry. In the sixteenth century Jews of German and Italian origin were forced to leave in what was the Island of the New Bell Foundry (*Ghetto* derives from the word in Venetian dialect *geto* pronounced with a German accent). Later the areas were the Jews were forced to live was extended to include the street were the old Bell Foundry used to be located. So the Ghetto Vecchio (literally Old Ghetto) was the first extension and the Ghetto Nuovo (literally New Ghetto) the original. It may sound weird. After all, it is a Venetian and Jewish concept, therefore not weird at all !
2. Broadly speaking Shabbat starts 18 minutes before sunset on Friday and ends after sunset on Saturday. In Venice in January it would sometimes between 5 and 6pm on Saturday afternoon.
3. The Jewish New Year. In 1916 Rosh Hashanah fell on 29 September.

Chapter 14

1. Coming of age ceremony that Jewish boys go through when they are thirteen. Traditionally it involves reading either from the scrolls of the Torah or from a Haftarah. The Hebrew text is usually read with a chant that may differ from one local tradition to another.

Chapter 16

1. The name of the table where the scrolls of the law are placed when the law is read in Synagogue.

About the Author

Silvano Stagni is a multilingual citizen of the world, a father of four, a cosmopolitan character with a long and varied life. In his youth, he was blessed to have many storytellers, people from different cultures and walks of life. He heard stories from the Imperial Court in Vienna, stories from the Kenyan bush, stories of seafarers, stories of survivors, and stories of fighters. He started writing articles, white papers and opinion pieces during his previous professional life as an expert in the implementation of financial regulations. Now it is his turn to tell stories.